THE SKULLS OF
MALGRANGE
AN EDWARD TYRINGTON MYSTERY
- BOOK 2
JONI SWIFT

SPIRANTE PRESS

For C.
Who changed my life just by being.
Thank you for being your authentic self.

Contents

Chapter One	1
Chapter Two	7
Chapter Three	12
Chapter Four	15
Chapter Five	19
Chapter Six	25
Chapter Seven	31
Chapter Eight	39
Chapter Nine	45
Chapter Ten	51
Chapter Eleven	59
Chapter Twelve	65
Chapter Thirteen	73
Chapter Fourteen	77
Chapter Fifteen	81
Chapter Sixteen	89

Chapter Seventeen	95
Chapter Eighteen	100
Chapter Nineteen	110
Chapter Twenty	116
Chapter Twenty One	121
Chapter Twenty Two	128
Chapter Twenty Three	132
Chapter Twenty Four	135
Chapter Twenty Five	140
Chapter Twenty Six	146
Chapter Twenty Seven	152
Chapter Twenty Eight	157
Chapter Twenty Nine	162
Chapter Thirty	169
Chapter Thirty One	177
Chapter Thirty Two	183
Chapter Thirty Three	188
Chapter Thirty Four	195
Chapter Thirty Five	200
Chapter Thirty Six	205
Chapter Thirty Seven	210
Chapter Thirty Eight	216

Chapter Thirty Nine   223

Chapter Forty   228

Chapter Forty One   232

Chapter Forty Two   237

Chapter Forty Three   244

Chapter Forty Four   250

Chapter Forty Five   255

Chapter Forty Six   260

Chapter Forty Seven   266

Chapter Forty Eight   272

Chapter Forty Nine   278

Acknowledgements   284

CHAPTER ONE

September 1863—Paris, France

The morning was unusually hot for September. As Catherine stood before Edward at the entrance to his archaeological site, a rush of inconsequential words rushed from her soft mouth as if the Devil was behind her and she was trying not to notice. She asked about the whys and hows of his arrival and met all his answers with an anxious smile.

Edward had tried to avoid her, even though she lived here in Paris. He had told no one except his best friend Henri that he was working here, but perhaps it had just been a matter of time before she found out where he was working and came to visit him.

Her reddish-gold curls glinted in the shifting sun as they cascaded past her shoulders, and her royal-blue dress amplified the hurricane color of her eyes: a calm of crystal blue within a stormy circle of dark gray. He was pleased that after several courting seasons without a match, she had neither descended into the lack of care of a woman who has given up nor sought the overly taut waspish waist of a woman trying too hard. She was, to put it succinctly, exactly as he remembered her.

The small talk she was forcing him to engage in, however, was not normal for her. Typically, her conversation was consequential. As a woman who surreptitiously ran her father's shipping business, the words she used were economical and chosen for maximum clarity and efficiency. She spoke in ways that mattered about topics that mattered, and Edward wondered why she spewed such fluff now.

His hand throbbed, and he mulled over the possibility that he was already suffering ill effects from his recent wound. His grip tightened on the handkerchief around his hand, and he tried to remember what he knew of blood poisoning symptoms—or ancient curses, for that matter. He chided himself for being foolish and tried to focus on what Catherine was saying. He could not quite believe that she was here at his archaeological dig. Amid her uncharacteristic chatter, he realized that despite how trying he remembered her to be, he had missed her quite a lot.

Edward's attention snapped back to the moment as Catherine asked, "Why is there no one here?"

Edward sighed. "My entire excavation crew walked off the job. More like ran off the job."

"What?" She spun around and surveyed the deserted excavation entrance. "Why?"

Edward unwrapped his hand, which still smarted, and held it out for her inspection. "Because of this."

She looked at the stab wound on the side of his palm. "That? It does not appear to be so dire."

It offended Edward that she was so dismissive. "The sword of a skeleton guard stabbed me. My blood ran on his thousand-year-old blade. The workers spoke of a curse and ran. It was an amateurish mistake on my part."

"Nonsense. Besides, there is no scientific evidence of curses. That is...—"

"There are many stories in the archaeological community, anecdotal evidence of archaeologists dying from unknown diseases or being mauled by animals after excavating a burial chamber such as this. My crew believes I am a dead man already."

She shuddered and straightened. "Surely you do not believe that."

Edward loosely replaced his bloody handkerchief around the wound and stuffed his hand back into his pocket. "It does not matter what I believe. There will be no further excavation until I can find a new crew or I die, whichever comes first."

She inhaled sharply, and Edward noticed that she looked paler than he remembered. She was not the typical Englishwoman who eschewed the sun at all costs. Despite the recent end of summer, her pallor was ghostly. She coughed.

The rising wind blew the dust from the excavation, and the brown leaves that had already fallen were tumbling in circles in the square outside the dig's entrance. A nearby woman struggled with her parasol, which threatened to snap in the gust of wind. The vegetable stand owners along the Seine were looking at the sky and scurrying to pack up their stands. Edward pointed to the east end of the square. "Let us move out of the wind." He guided her around the corner to a small, sheltered café. The smell of strong coffee and sweet croissants relaxed his shoulders as he inhaled. He ordered an espresso and *pain au chocolat* with two plates, knowing that although Catherine refused to order, she would want a small portion. He was glad to share.

"You said you had something to tell me."

She swung her head back and forth, as if she were looking around to find another place to sit. "Perhaps we should go to your home. I can tell you there."

Edward fidgeted with impatience, unwrapped his hand and dabbed at the stab wound again. To his consternation, it kept bleeding. He leaned toward her. "What is it?"

She avoided his eyes, staring at her own handkerchief, which she twisted mercilessly between her fingers. "Edward, there is no way to say this gently, and I only wish it were untrue..." She drew a deep breath. "Henri is dead."

The shock of her words shook Edward. Everything slowed. His brain could not process what he heard. Henri was his best friend.

He looked up to search Catherine's face and found the truth there. Her eyes were red-rimmed and puffy, her cheeks and nose were ruddy from crying. How had he not noticed before? His thoughts continued at a snail's pace. *He cannot be dead. He said he would only be away for a few weeks. How could he be... I need him. Damn you, Edward. A decent man would think of his friend's family's loss. A decent man would mourn his friend's shortened life, but you only think of yourself.*

He cast his gaze from the café and saw a park bench near the river with fallen leaves blowing around it. The bench was gray and weathered and reminded him of the freezing park benches where he had sat alone to watch the sunsets after his father died. No one had called on him during his mourning. Except for Henri's occasional presence, he had spent a year as a hermit watching sunsets alone along the river every evening, trying to put together the pieces of his father's life, which had left him a pauper. It was Henri who had gotten him his archaeological job with the Suez Canal Company. Now, looking at the empty bench by the river, he saw a cold carpet of lonely days stretch before him, and his heart ached.

"There must be some mistake. How?"

Catherine swallowed hard. "He was...shot. He was with his cousin Evaline's husband Davet, who was also..." The words hung there, no conclusion, no reason, the most painful words simply left unspoken.

Edward's mind clung to cold facts to hold the sorrow in abeyance. He focused on finding all the reasons she might be wrong. "Where was this? Are they sure it was Henri? Has someone from the family identified him? It might be someone else."

Catherine shook her head. "I am so very sorry. Evaline identified them both. Henri's father and Joelle have already left for the town of Nancy, where it happened, to find out more." She looked at her hands on the table, then continued, "I think we should go to Nancy to investigate."

Panic rose within him, and his throat tightened. He could not sit with her and make plans; the need to move was visceral and immediate. He stood. "I have to go."

"What? Where?"

He dropped money on the table and left her sitting alone.

CHAPTER TWO

As he jogged back to his excavation of Roman ruins, a gust of wind snatched at his hat. He grabbed it and held it to his chest. In the darkening morning sky, he gazed up at the towers of Notre Dame, the stained-glass windows filled with colorful angels and saints lit from within by prayerful candles. The clouds advanced downward, one layer below another, grazing the top of the cathedral spire like ghostly monks descending from the heavens to wash the city clean. Edward cursed God, but then thought better of it.

He climbed down the worn wooden ladder into the excavation to his small office there. The air was cooler and less humid down here. The floor mosaic of a black dog with his tail up, his forelegs bent, and his teeth bared, seemed more menacing now. Cave Canem, "Beware the dog," it said. He lit as many lamps as he could to push away the fear and pain that took turns swiping at his heart, and then properly stored the tools dropped by the workers who had rushed to leave after his injury. A curse was easier to face than his grief. Once he had tidied a bit, he took a lantern and walked deeper into the excavation. The main corridor crept back into the darkness, with rough-hewn stone walls along either side of the narrow passage. His lantern light pushed deeper below ground, and the walls came closer as he went.

The sloping floor was smooth, and the low ceiling caused him to crouch.

Fifty feet from where he entered, he saw the first skeletons. Each lay on a berth carved into the rock wall. He placed his lantern on the floor. There were four berths from bottom to top on each side of the hallway, and all eight skeletons lay flat with their hands crossed on their chests. Each had a sword that had been clasped in their hands at burial, and each had the remnants of a belt of leather and brass.

He went to the skeleton that cut him. The point of his rusted sword remained sharp. Edward took his kerchief, wiped his blood from the blade, and continued on.

The passage was narrowest here, not quite shoulder width across, and he followed it for another twenty feet. At the end of the corridor, Edward stepped into a large room with a vaulted ceiling. There was brickwork for the ribs of each of the four vaults that came together to form the roof. Edward held his lantern high and observed the white plaster and frescoes between the brick ribs. The faded colors showed Mary and Joseph and the baby Jesus in a fresco on the left with angels floating around them on clouds, St. Paul in blue robes with a lamb was on the right, and the central vault across from the hallway contained a fresco of Jesus on the cross.

Edward knelt on the ground, his knees protesting the press of the cold, hard stone. He faced Jesus on the cross, and the angels watched as he prayed for the first time since his mother died so many years ago. *Please, dear God, do not let Henri be dead. Please let this be some terrible mistake. I will do whatever service or penance I must, but Henri must be...* His thoughts broke in a flood of tears as he curled himself up in a ball on the floor. He had already lost so many people: his mother, his father, his brother Thaddeus, and now his best friend. It seemed he should be used to grief, but beneath the tears and pleading, he felt a howling loneliness. A loneliness that consumed him in its maw, with one death-filled bite after another.

His eyes fell on his shirt buttons. They were set with mother-of-pearl and onyx that had been a Christmas gift from Henri their senior year at Oxford. Henri visited them at the Tyrington family's Essex estate over the holiday. It had been bitterly cold that winter, but they had fun having snowball fights and sledding down the narrow country lane that led to the estate.

Edward sighed. What were Henri's last moments like? Were they filled with fear, or anger, or fighting?

Edward recalled his father's praise of Henri, even as he chided Edward, and thought how saddened Lord Tyrington would be to hear of Henri's death—if he had not predeceased him. Edward pushed away the jealousy that lingered around his father's relationship with Henri. He thought instead of how Henri's eyes would sparkle with mischief as he brought the women of the bawdy houses flowers as if he were a suitor. Occasionally the women had mistaken Edward for Henri when he walked in the seedier side of town after dark. Some had remarked they looked like twins with their dark curls to their collars, their firm jaws, and their broad shoulders. The similarity ended with their noses. Henri's was larger with a rather noticeable bump in the middle, while Edward's was smaller and more refined, Roman even. Regardless, they were mistaken as brothers more often than not.

He wiped his eyes. A powerful gust of wind blew down the passage, and the light in his lantern stuttered. He pulled himself together. This was the last place he wanted to be stuck in the dark. He returned to the entrance and placed as many large rocks as he could to seal off the hall. When finished, he sat at his desk and dashed off a quick note to Henri's mother to request a visit that evening, then went to the Sorbonne to tell his employer that his crew had walked off the job.

After a curt conversation with his benefactors, they agreed a hiatus was unavoidable and they would replace his crew as quickly as possible. In the meantime, he would be without a job. Edward thought of his bills and hoped he could borrow just a bit more from his brother Charles. Charles had inherited the estate in Essex and although he, too, was in less than stellar financial shape, the estate provided an income for him, as did his seat in the House of Lords. He had plenty of money, but he was as miserly as Scrooge himself and lectured Edward every time he borrowed, even though Edward routinely paid him back.

The archaeological entrance had a medium sized building with a doorway built over the opening at the surface with a steep set of stairs leading down into the excavation. Edward locked the door and closed the fence and as he left, the rain came, soaking his coat. The chilly drops mingled with his hot tears, and he felt he could cry in peace as he walked home through the storm, his grief on display and yet hidden.

His man Davis greeted him at the door and quickly found him a towel. "Good afternoon, sir. You are soaked. Were there no cabs?

Did the rain end your work early today?" Davis had been his father's valet before becoming his, and over the years he had become something more akin to a confidant.

Edward sighed. "Davis, please stop fussing over me. I have bad news. There is no good way to say this, but I suggest you sit down."

Davis sat on the plush green velvet couch across from the fireplace, and Edward went to the spirits table, his shoes leaving a trail of wet footprints, which he noticed Davis watching. He poured them both a whiskey. Handing a glass to Davis, Edward said, "Henri is dead."

CHAPTER THREE

Davis had known Henri since Napoleon III had forced Henri's family to live in exile in London. He looked aghast at Edward's news. "What?"

"I wish it was not so, but it seems he was murdered, along with his cousin Evaline's husband, Davet. Evaline identified him."

Davis sat in silence, trying to grasp the news. Edward drank his whiskey in one go then removed his coat and boots. Davis raised his glass before him, silently toasting Henri, and drank. Edward turned away and let Davis have a moment. Davis had always been good to Henri, and Edward recalled the slight gestures he had made to make Henri's life in exile easier. He would purchase books written in French and leave them in Henri's room at the Essex estate. He even encouraged the cook to make coq au vin and crêpes. Edward's father had not bid Davis to do these things but supported him when he did. Davis had grown up as an Irish boy in England, so he understood exile better than most and was committed to easing Henri's plight. Henri had been an unofficial member of Edward's family, and Edward knew the news devastated Davis.

As Edward poured more whiskey, Davis asked, "Why is your hand wrapped, sir?"

"The sword of a skeletal guard stabbed me today at our excavation. My crew left out of fear of an ancient curse. I am currently without a job until we replace them."

Davis stood and retrieved his sleek black leather medical kit from the bedroom then directed Edward to sit at the dining room table. He placed bottles, a scalpel, and cotton batting between them. One of the enduring legacies of Edward's father was that he had bribed University College at London to educate Davis in the medical arts to keep Edward safe during his archaeological travels. This was a considerable gift, considering how his father disapproved of Edward's chosen profession. Edward's father had told Davis it was his most important task, and Davis continued to treat it as such, frequently reading medical journals to stay abreast of the latest techniques.

Edward noted Davis's jaw was set in determination and suspected his tending Edward's wound was a way to avoid thinking about Henri.

"Davis, you do not need to attend to me."

Ignoring him, Davis asked, "Have you cleaned the wound?"

Edward held out his hand for inspection. "Yes, with the bottle of weak carbolic acid you gave me."

Davis nodded and inspected his hand. "Was the blade rusted?"

Edward's mind turned back to the darkness of his excavation. All the blades were rusted, as well as the belt buckles. "Yes, the blade is likely over a thousand years old."

Davis shuddered slightly, no doubt imagining all the things besides rust that could have been on the blade. He swabbed alcohol on the cut with a clean square of cloth, then took his scalpel and reopened the wound. Blood sprang forth as Edward winced. He hissed as Davis irrigated it with carbolic acid again.

"Was that necessary?" Edward spat through clenched teeth.

Davis's eyes bored into Edward's with a fire that clearly said to never question him about medicine. Edward knew anatomy, but Davis understood healing. Edward looked away and closed his mouth.

Davis replied, "Lockjaw is a possibility here. Bleeding and cleaning are the only tools we have to prevent it. If you notice any tremors, fever, chills, or stiffness of the neck or jaw, you must inform me immediately."

"Why? So you can watch me die?"

Davis visibly flinched at Edward's quip. While Edward regretted his boorish remark, in this moment, the prospect of death did not seem so bad.

Davis finished bandaging Edward's hand using gauze and alcohol. "Please stop being maudlin. It is unlikely, but we must be sure."

After he put his medicine kit away, Davis stoked the fire in the large stone fireplace, added another heavy oak log, and ordered Edward to sit before it. As Edward sat drinking whiskey and trying to resist his grief, he received a response from Henri's mother instructing him to arrive at nine o'clock, well past normal visiting hours. The late invitation perplexed him, but it gave him more time to prepare himself.

CHAPTER FOUR

That evening, as his carriage approached the le Marchal mansion near the center of Paris, his heart sank at the black crepe that draped the windows and doors. The billowy, floating fabric cemented his loss. The butler hastened Edward to Alfonse le Marchal's library. Edward recalled Alphonse explaining the hidden messages the decor here conveyed: the royal-blue rug, the white marble floor, the red furnishings, the obscure relics and objets d'art linked to France's history. Everything in the room represented his love of France. After the family's return from exile, it seemed prudent to show off his fealty to his country. Alfonse had told Edward that some of his cohorts in the National Assembly had remarked on it when they visited, while others were oblivious. Those who noticed were Alfonse's closest friends. Looking around, Edward wondered how anyone could miss the symbolism, and he mused over how many dullards there likely were in the National Assembly. The room was overly warm, with a fire roaring in the large white marble fireplace. A feeling of claustrophobia gripped him.

Madame le Marchal stood from a chair in the darkest corner of the room. He hadn't noticed her at first, and her rising like a black ghost startled him. She crossed to him like a bloodless apparition, silent and watchful. The blackness of her wig and dress were stark against her almost translucent skin. As she approached, she slowly lifted her hand. Her entire demeanor gave Edward the impression she might blow away into a puff of smoke and slide up the chimney. Her voice, however, belied her apparent otherworldliness with a whiskey-tuned timber that he remembered fondly.

"Edward, thank you so much for coming." It was unsettling to see her so shrunken. This was not the robust woman he remembered, and it gave him pause.

She invited him to sit across from her by the fire. He removed his jacket before he sat, and shared his condolences for her loss. Then he said, "If I may ask, what happened? Why was he in Nancy?"

"He was visiting Evaline and Davet. He said he had some work to do there, but he did not share what it was. We do not know what happened other than they were both..." Her sentence hung in the air as if its lack of ending would somehow bring Henri back alive. It annoyed Edward that both Catherine and now Madame le Marchal did this. No amount of superstitious refusal to say that he died would bring him back. She continued, "Alfonse and Joelle confirmed his identity. They are planning to bring... bring..." She bit her trembling lip and squeezed her eyes shut against the pain of the words. Edward knew she was trying to say: "bring him home." She drew a deep breath, opened her eyes, and again continued, "The funeral will be on Sunday. Alfonse has decided it will be a small affair."

He knelt before her and took her hand. "I am so sorry. Henri was like a brother to me. Please know that I will do all I can for you and your family."

Her coal-black eyes widened as if a demon possessed her soul. The roaring fire reflected in them was startling and evil and made Edward hold his breath. There had been some madness in the ancestral women of Henri's family, Edward knew, and for a moment he questioned whether the shock of losing her son had pushed her among their ranks. His thoughts were interrupted as she commanded him. It was a command only she could give.

"Find who did this. Find them and make them pay."

Edward felt dizzy for a moment. "Surely your family has other, more professional means of finding the perpetrator."

"Bah. The French police will do nothing for a family of former exiles, despite Alfonse being back in his rightful place in the National Assembly." Her voice dropped to a whisper. "I expect no help from our government, and I have not ruled them out as responsible. I think that may be why Alfonse has dictated a small funeral. There is something afoot, but I do not know what it is. No one tells me anything. They try to protect me. I need you, Edward. I need someone who knows Henri but who is also an outsider to the French government. Only you can find who did this. Please tell me you will find them. Please. After Greece, you owe him this much."

Edward sighed and stared into the flames. It was true. Henri had saved his life in Greece, in no uncertain terms. He lifted his countenance and returned her gaze. "I will do my best. I only fear it will not be enough."

She straightened in her chair and gave him an imperious look. "Then you must do better, because you are all I have."

Edward felt as though he were making a deal with the devil, an impossible deal that he could never uphold, but he loved Henri and his family. He kissed her hands and touched them to his forehead. "I will travel to Nancy after the funeral."

She shook her head. "After the funeral will be too late. You must leave tomorrow. Go see Evaline and find out what you can." She pulled her hands away and bustled to the desk. "I took the liberty of writing you a letter of introduction. Give this to Evaline so she knows what I have asked of you."

Edward took the letter and left.

CHAPTER FIVE

E dward stood outside the le Marchal mansion and hailed a carriage. The cool air of fall was refreshing after sitting in front of the fire. He directed the driver to a corner near Henri's house on rue des Innocents. Henri always thought it was a great joke to live on "Innocent Street," being one of the least "innocent" people he knew. The last time Edward was there, when he first arrived in Paris, he remarked to Henri that his house seemed rather small and out of the way. There were none of the usual amusements that Henri liked to surround himself with: bars, theaters, women of questionable moral standing. He had exhibited great restraint in Egypt and Greece, as these entertainments were less available, but in Paris, his home, they were plentiful—seemingly everywhere except where Henri lived. Henri declared that was by design and would hear no more discussion of relocating to a more interesting or upstanding part of town. Edward had wondered if Henri was trying to reform himself, or if he was hiding from something, or someone.

As the carriage turned onto rue des Innocents, the street struck Edward as dark and ominously quiet. There was another apartment house across the street from Henri's, its chipping clapboard facade looking tired and warped, and a small cobbler's shop next door had a faded "Rooms to Let" sign that hung at an odd angle. All the buildings were dark. He alighted from the carriage and waited at the corner for a few minutes to watch the area. After another lone carriage passed, he turned toward Henri's. The road was rough, with cobblestones jutting up at odd angles. He walked carefully and waited in the alley next to the building for a few more minutes.

As he turned toward Henri's door, he saw a person out of the corner of his eye. He froze until Catherine gave a low wave. Pulling out his lockpicks, he worked the door by feel and opened it as she joined him on the stoop. They both slipped inside.

He saw a coat hanging on the hook, waiting for Henri to come wear it again, as if he had only gone out for a moment. The finality that he would never return to this house broke his heart. Edward remembered him wearing that coat when he had visited the Essex estate last summer. Henri never invested himself in seriously courting, but during that visit, he mentioned one woman's name far more than the others. Edward grasped for the wispy memory but could not conjure her name. Perhaps it was Marie, perhaps Marta? Marie felt more correct. Although Edward did not remark on it at the time, as it would cause Henri to never say her name again, Edward wondered if their connection had lasted and where she was now. *Did she know? Did she care? Or was she in the envious position of believing Henri would return to her one day, her dreams of future visits still intact, unlike his own?*

He turned to Catherine with his finger on his lips and then drew the living room shades closed. "I knew you would follow me," he whispered as he struck a match and found a candle to light. "What on earth are you doing here?"

Catherine straightened. "I was not following you. I simply surmised you would come here, and I never got the chance to tell you how sorry I am about Henri."

Edward set the candle down. "I apologize for leaving you at the café, I just...well..." He hung his head and sighed, then followed with a stern warning. "But you should not be out alone at night, especially in this neighborhood."

"I am following the terms of our previous agreement and only investigating when I am with you."

Edward walked away, raking his hands through his hair, and hissed, "You should not be investigating at all."

"Then why are you here?"

Edward looked through the mail on the hall table. "This is not an investigation."

Catherine crossed her arms, incredulity scrawled across her pursed lips and raised eyebrows.

He continued, "All right, it is an investigation. Madame le Marchal has charged me with finding the perpetrator and bringing him to justice."

"How do you know it is not a woman?"

Edward opened a drawer and pulled out two rings of keys, a bill for a new suit marked as paid, and business cards from a tailor and a cobbler. "My God, I forgot how trying you can be. While I appreciate your insistence that I not limit the field too early, perhaps you can refrain from reminding me how evil women can be—for the next few minutes, at least."

Catherine nibbled her lower lip before she wandered into the living room and sat. "I cannot believe it." She inhaled sharply. "His house still smells like him. He always smelled faintly of almonds."

Edward closed his eyes and took a deep breath. He smelled the faint hint of almond from Henri's hair pomade and also the scent of orange blossoms. Henri had orange blossom oil added to his sealing wax so his letters would smell "refreshing." More recently, he had the oil added to his candles. Edward sniffed the nearest candle, and the citrus infusion filled his nostrils.

He couldn't bear to think of Henri's death while standing in his house. "Catherine, please do not remark on him right now. I need to concentrate, and your commentary is not helpful."

Catherine returned to the hall. "What are you looking for?"

"Anything out of the ordinary. Anything that might show what he was doing in Nancy or who he was working for."

After they searched the living room and kitchen and found nothing, they moved upstairs. The stairs were narrow and steep, and the worn wallpaper had a faded red fleur-de-lis pattern in velvet. Edward walked ahead with the candle and took Catherine's hand to keep her from falling in the darkness behind him. Her hand felt abnormally cold, and he instinctively squeezed it to help the blood flow. She pulled her hand back and held the skirt of her black chiffon dress as she climbed the stairs. Her dress was the color of mourning, with a small white love ribbon at the base of her throat. Edward disliked it immensely.

He entered the room on the left and closed the draperies. It was Henri's bedroom. He noted the stark juxtaposition of the old wallpaper that was peeling near the edges with the high-quality furniture. There was a large oak sleigh-style bed, and an oak armoire with birds engraved near the top. Built-in bookshelves lined one wall. Edward went to the armoire while Catherine looked beneath the bed.

"Oh, a coil spring bed. Those are quite expensive."

Edward quipped, "We are not here to appraise the furniture. Perhaps you should wait in the hall."

Catherine made a sour face at him and perused the books while Edward picked the lock on the armoire. It contained two suits on hangers, with shirts and sundries within the interior drawers. He checked under all the clothes but found nothing unexpected. He pulled out the drawers one by one and lifted them overhead to see if Henri had attached anything to the bottom. Underneath the bottom drawer, a silver key glinted in the flickering candlelight. "Hello. What are you?"

Catherine came over. "What do you suppose it is the key to?"

"I do not know, but look at it. It is not a typical passkey. This key is flat with a jagged edge; it will only fit a tumbler lock. Whatever this key goes to, it is something Henri wants to keep absolutely secure. Look around for a lock that is round and that you cannot see through the hole." Edward pocketed the key and opened a large cedar chest at the foot of the bed.

Catherine returned to the bookshelves and removed one. "I am surprised Henri would have such a puritanical book as *Social Dynamite.*"

"I have never heard of it. What is it?"

"A book on the ills of a more relaxed society. For example, our situation here alone in a bedroom and unwed would be grounds for the author to keel over dead from the impropriety of it."

"This *is* highly improper, and any other woman would have more of a care with her reputation."

"My reputation can only be harmed if people know about my activities." Opening the book cover, she continued, "Ah, his aunt gave it to him. That makes far more sense."

Edward moved to the nightstand and pulled the contents from each drawer. There were buttons, a comb, a ring of skeleton keys, and a picture of a woman. It was blurry, as if she had moved during the exposure, but her smile was engaging.

As he looked at the picture, Catherine said, "Edward..."

He turned, and she was holding the open book in her left hand and a torn slip of paper in her right.

CHAPTER SIX

Edward crossed to Catherine. The book in her hand had the center pages cut out to create a secret hole, and she was studying the slip of paper she'd found inside. "This is a portion of a ship's manifest."

She handed it to him. The paper was soft, as if many people had handled it. The portion of the sheet listed several items, including twenty-two bolts of cotton, three pallets of chair spindles and four elephants.

"Elephants?" she asked. "Who on earth would ship elephants?"

"It could be jewelry, ivory, or a code word for contraband."

"What else can you tell me about this shipment?"

"Not much. All the important details are at the top of the manifest, which is missing."

They searched the other books for secret compartments, but finding none, they moved to the next upstairs room.

In Henri's office, they found a rolltop desk that only contained a pen and ink set, a few coins, and a half-written letter. It spoke of the weather and the possibility of a le Marchal hunt at their estate in Avignon later in the year, but nothing of consequence.

"Does it seem odd that he left on an extended trip and did not complete this letter to his cousin Andrew?" Edward asked.

"No. Henri dislikes him. His mother was likely pushing him to write. You know how Henri can be when his mother badgers him."

It discomfited him that Catherine had such familiarity with Henri's personality and his family. His mind wandered into the dangerous territory of whether there was more to Catherine and Henri's relationship than met the eye. His mind conjured a picture of her smiling in Henri's arms. He sighed and pushed the image away. Their relationship was none of his business, or at least he told himself that as he stuffed his clawing jealousy into the darkest corner of his mind. The Briggses had spent several summers visiting the le Marchals many years ago. He tried to comfort himself that they were like siblings as he searched the remaining drawers in the desk. He found nothing abnormal, so he moved to the small closet on the far side of the room. It contained a few winter overcoats and a stack of hatboxes. Edward opened the boxes and found several hats, including a monstrosity of ribbons and ostrich feathers masquerading as a lady's hat. Holding it aloft, he asked, "Who would he have purchased this for?"

Catherine physically repulsed when she saw it. "Aunt Agnes. She relishes such atrocities in fashion."

As Edward was returning the hat to the box, his fingers brushed against a stack of papers hidden inside: manifests. He handed them to Catherine. She rifled through them, removed one, and handed it back to Edward. "These are all cargo manifests and passenger lists from ships owned by Gaston Bergeron."

"Who is that?"

"A shipping magnate. Our chief competitor. He is as infamous as he is immoral. Perhaps Henri has been working for Bergeron or one of his clients."

Edward pulled all the remaining boxes from the closet and made two additional finds: a signet ring with a hinged lid for storage, and a bottle of liquid. The signet was not the le Marchal's. He handed this also to Catherine. "Do you recognize this signet?"

"No, but these are hard to read backward." She pressed the ring into the soft wax around the base of the candle holder. The imprint was a shield with three fleur-de-lis. "I have never seen this crest." She handed the ring back to Edward, who pocketed it, along with the stack of shipping manifests.

There was a sharp knock on the front door.

Edward and Catherine froze. A second knock came, more insistent this time, and a man yelled, "I know you're in there. I saw the candlelight through the gap in the curtains."

Edward took the candle and hastened down the stairs with Catherine at his heels.

"May I help you?" Edward said as he opened the door.

An older man pushed past him and stood in the front hall. His gray hair was bushy and unkempt, and he was unshaven. He looked as though he had come straight from bed. He was rather rotund, and he smelled of a mixture of beef and beer.

"Where's Monsieur le Marchal?"

"Who are you?"

"I'm his landlord. Who are you?"

Without giving it much thought, but realizing that this man likely did not know of Henri's fate, Edward thrust out his hand. "I am his cousin, Edward Sinclair, and this is my sister Regina. Henri asked us to retrieve an address from his desk. I am to wire it to him."

"Why didn't he ask his father for that? He was here yesterday."

Edward laughed, "I do not know." Then pushing his way toward the door, "But it is rather late, and we need to be going. Sorry to have disturbed you."

The man grabbed his arm. "Not so fast. Henri has never mentioned you to me before. What did you say your name was again?"

"Sinclair. I am his second cousin. If you know Henri at all, you know he has quite a lot of cousins."

The man leaned in and inspected his face. "I see a family resemblance, but you don't have his nose."

"Yes, well, thank the Lord for minor miracles." Edward chuckled and continued, "Please excuse us. I need to return to Uncle Alphonse and Aunt Suzette."

The man nodded. "I know those names. You have a pleasant night, then. And remind them that his rent is due next week." The landlord escorted them from the house and locked the door behind them.

Edward and Catherine hastened a few blocks away in silence before hailing a cab. A chilly breeze made the night uncomfortable, and Edward was happy to hurry. Catherine eventually tugged on his sleeve and slowed her pace. Between breaths she said, "Your sister? We look nothing alike."

"A fact he failed to notice. I was trying to have a care of your reputation. Would you rather I had told him your real name?"

"Of course not, but if he had looked at me at all, he might have noticed I was not your sister."

Edward stopped as a realization froze his heart. "I apologize. It occurs to me that in my haste to protect your reputation, I may have inadvertently implied that you are my mistress."

Catherine looked at him agog, and Edward continued, "By calling you my sister, I may have surreptitiously asked him to exercise discretion regarding my mistress. That is the way of the French, is it not? For a man to call his mistress his sister to strangers? I promise it was not my intention."

Edward braced himself for the onslaught to come, but Catherine threw her head back in a deep belly laugh that only grew louder and less restrained. It was clearly cathartic for Catherine to laugh this hard. As she calmed herself, she said, "Oh my. That is...quite...something. After all your statements of protecting my reputation," she continued laughing, "I never want to hear another word about my carelessness."

He laughed with her for a few more moments before his thoughts turned to Henri, and a part of him wanted to blunt her frivolity. As he held up a hand to hail a carriage, the words were out of his mouth before he considered them.

"I am planning on going to Nancy. I do not know what I will find, or when I will return."

Catherine did not respond, but he saw her deflate, her laughter silenced. Only the curt words of "Good night" were exchanged as she entered the carriage and left him on the curb to walk home.

CHAPTER SEVEN

The next day, Edward arrived at Catherine's office north of the Seine at ten in the morning to see if she had discovered anything about the shipment of elephants. The sun was out, and it seemed everyone who had the time was enjoying the river. Lovers, grandparents with small children, even workers were in the river park. The warmth of the sun on his coat coaxed his spirits from their inky blackness as he opened the door to Briggs Shipping.

The cacophony inside immediately stunned him. It appeared that all of humanity was here, many of them shouting. A young man yelled and handed a paper to a small runner who sprinted across the room, weaving between the crowds of men as if he were a shuttle on a loom. Except for those waiting to be served, the entire room seemed to emit an air of efficient chaos. Each movement seemed choreographed to be quick and repetitive. Even the runners, who at first seemed haphazard as they scurried about, were following well-worn paths to each desk. Although they seemed rushed, they did not seem flustered. It was clear this was just how they did things every day. It was a well-managed tumult.

Someone pushed past him as they entered, and he shook himself from his reverie. Edward saw a large mahogany desk in the center of the room marked "Information." He asked the gentleman if Miss Briggs was available. As a boy passed, the older man called to him, "Visitor for Miss Briggs."

Edward said, "Edward Tyrington," and realized his voice was lost in the room's hum.

The young man barely slowed his pace then disappeared behind a door. He returned a few minutes later and handed Edward a note.

Please meet me in fifteen minutes at the wire office on Rue de Castiglioni.

Edward left for the office, and Catherine arrived ten minutes later. Of all the apparent bedlam of her office, Catherine seemed to be the most in disarray. He saw her hurry down the street, her black hat askew and her hair slightly mussed. Her heavy breathing stripped away her normal composure. Edward had a brief remembrance of trying to run while wearing a corset and was in awe of her as he pushed the memory away.

She breathlessly approached him. "I apologize, but I need to send a telegraph, and I am meeting my father for a late breakfast. It has been a trying morning. Wait here. I will only be a moment." When she returned, she had straightened her hair and hat and she had regained her composure. "Will you join us? He would love to see you." She pointed to a restaurant with seating overlooking the water and walked in the café's direction.

Edward asked, "Your father still believes we are courting?"

A breeze blew gently off the river, bringing the laughter of children and the honking of ducks begging for food. She looked toward the river and the children playing in the sun.

"Yes."

Edward followed her gaze and saw two young boys fishing. It reminded him of his afternoons at the Essex estate with Henri. They would frequently catch their dinner and take it to the kitchen to be prepared for the guests. He turned his head away and forced himself to focus on the conversation.

"Then no. How did I ever let you convince me to keep up that charade?"

"It was a great kindness that you did."

Edward's voice took on an accusing tone. "To him or to you."

She stopped and faced him, and the tide of pedestrians parted around them like waves around a jetty, jostling and rearranging themselves. "To both of us. Admittedly, I benefit from the lack of scrutiny, since he believes it is only a matter of time before I am married. However, his health has taken many turns, and I firmly believe he would be worse off worrying about my future."

Edward gazed down at his shoes. "I am sorry to hear that, but I feel guilty about deceiving him, as should you."

Catherine turned to face forward. "I do, but I continue to believe it is the right course."

They walked again, and Edward changed the subject. "Can you tell me anything else about the manifests we found, or the ring?"

"I reviewed the manifests, and there were three shipments of elephants, all from India. The remaining shipments, by rail, contained a host of other products, but none seemed odd. However, the amount of space allocated to the elephants was rather large. These took up a space one might imagine a real elephant would require. I checked, and there was no sign that they provided any food or care, so we can assume these were not actual elephants."

"What about the ring?"

"I checked Debrett's Book of Peerage and found nothing on that seal. However, Debrett's focuses on English peers."

"How can Debrett's be touted as so exhaustive if they only list Englishmen?" Edward sighed.

Catherine gave him a sideways glance. "Nobody matters more to the British than the British."

The restaurant was small with intimate seating and the scent of fresh bread. Edward escorted her to the table by the window as John Briggs stood to welcome them. He looked worse than Edward remembered, with thinner hair and sunken eyes. His once vibrant color had faded until his hair, eyes, and skin all appeared a rather dull gray in the morning sunlight. His black suit hung off him as if he had lost weight, and his shoulders slumped forward with an air of sadness, as if he had one glorious plan in life that he no longer had the strength to meet. It was a shock, since it had only been a few months since Edward had last seen him.

After a brief reunion, Edward excused himself and left. He felt bad not taking time to visit with him, but his grief over Henri ensured he would be terrible company, and he did not have it in him to pretend to be courting Catherine and continue the lie they had arranged in Greece. There was some solace in knowing that Catherine was right; *If John looks that much worse without the worry of marrying off his daughter...* Edward shook his head. He did not want to finish the thought.

Edward spent the rest of the morning arranging his affairs and packing his trunk to leave Paris that evening. As much as he usually loved to travel, this trip was one he would rather not make. He did not know what he would be doing, or who he would be meeting, and therefore had trouble selecting outfits and items to bring. Davis was his usual efficient self and seemed to make several selections without informing Edward of them, which he was perfectly fine with. He pulled his Stradivarius from its case, held it to his chin, and plucked the strings experimentally. As he tuned it, there was a knock at the front door.

Davis went to answer it, and Edward heard Catherine's voice. Edward stood and went to the door of the study and invited her in. "What brings you here?"

Catherine had the same harried look as she'd had earlier in the morning, and she blurted, "I was discussing the shipment of elephants with my father at lunch. I mentioned finding some of Bergeron's receipts *somewhere*, and we discussed what it could mean."

"How could you, Catherine? We discussed that everything we found at Henri's would be our secret."

"No. You stated it should be so, I do not recall agreeing. Regardless, my father has made an appointment for you to speak to Bergeron."

"What? Without my consent?"

"It needed to be scheduled through an intermediary who was leaving this afternoon, and time was of the essence. I did not think you would mind."

"You did not think at all. Under what pretense am I to meet him?"

"As someone who is interested in shipping elephants, of course."

Edward's brows furrowed, and his jaw dropped. "Have you completely lost your faculties? We do not even know what elephants these are."

"I gave your name as Mr. Harrison, ivory merchant."

Edward rubbed his temples. "I do not know the first thing about ivory. How could you put me in this position? How am I supposed to have a conversation with this man on something about which I know nothing?"

"If he hired Henri to find or do something, then he may be the only one who might know what he was up to. I was not sure if he would meet with you to discuss any work Henri did for him. This way you can ask him in person to gauge his reaction. He will meet you at two o'clock at his home." She handed him a slip of paper with an address on it.

He exhaled, nodded, and slipped the paper into his pocket. "All right, but I think a more honest approach of simply asking after Henri might have been a better idea."

Shortly thereafter, Edward left to hail a carriage. Construction on several boulevards snarled traffic, and the delay only served to further sour Edward's mood. He did not know what to say to Bergeron and did not appreciate the ruse that had been created so he could speak to him.

As the carriage pulled into the approach of Gaston Bergeron's estate, Edward's courage seized. It was one thing to talk about visiting Bergeron and quite another to do it. Well-placed statuary lined the approach to his home, along with shrubs carved into the shapes of animals. There were few places in Paris that were this imposing. The drive climbed a hill through the forest, and Edward caught glimpses of the mansion through the trees as leaves showered across their path. Even obstructed, it appeared as a monstrous five-story structure with a mansard roof pierced by dormer windows. His father's Essex estate seemed small by comparison. The carriage crossed a covered bridge over a large stream before the final approach, which was lined with more statuary and topiary. Every segment of the drive to the house was designed to intimidate visitors and yet, as they continued to drive toward the house, Edward realized how superficial it was, as if the owner were trying too hard to intimidate his guests without realizing that, by such naked effort, he rendered the effect moot. Just as he was feeling less intimidated, the house came into full view. It was even larger than he had realized, and it intimidated Edward all over again.

He alighted from the cab and paid the driver to wait for him. He knocked on the door, and the butler answered.

Edward said, "Mr. Harrison to see Monsieur Bergeron."

The butler held a silver salver aloft to accept his card. Out of habit he reached for his own only to remember they said "Edward Tyrington." Removing his empty hand from his pocket, he patted and searched several other pockets. "I am terribly sorry, but I do not seem to have a calling card with me."

The butler's face was a study in cold marble as he showed Edward into a small study near the door and withdrew to announce him. The room was spare, almost spartan, in its furnishings, but each piece reflected impeccable taste and a sense of deliberation.

Chestnut paneling covered the walls, with tall diamond-paned windows that reached from floor to ceiling and afforded a view of an enormous expanse of lawn outside. The rugs were Persian in a deep ruby-and-gold pattern that shifted colors depending where you stood upon it, an effect created by the quality of the silk and the orientation of the weave. Edward recalled the first time he had seen this type of rug in the prime minister's residence. He was young at the time and recalled being transfixed by the effect. Edward snapped back to the present and took in the rest of the room. No two elements of the room had the same style; however, they created a harmony of color and placement with one another. The effect of each piece when compared with the last was jarring, but somehow the room felt warm and inviting, as if to say, *take a seat and the story of how this room came to be will unfold.*

Chapter Eight

The door of the study opened and Bergeron entered. He was quite short, at least half a foot shorter than Edward, but he seemed to make up for his lack of height with his aura of confidence. He was significantly younger than Edward had envisioned, perhaps forty years old, with a thick head of sandy blond hair, and his ruddy cheeks and red nose gave the impression of someone who is familiar with excess. His jacket strained at the buttons, showing a recent change in weight, but the clothes themselves were of impeccable material. Edward had assumed Bergeron would be closer to Mr. Briggs's age.

"Mr. Harrison. I am Gaston Bergeron. It is a pleasure to meet you."

Edward replied, "You as well."

Bergeron gestured to the sofa. "Please make yourself comfortable. May I offer you a whiskey?"

"Please." Edward sat. "But before you do, I should properly introduce myself. I regret to admit that I have presented myself under false pretenses."

Bergeron stepped away from the spirits table, his demeanor taking on a far more menacing tone. "Then who are you, and why are you here?"

Edward stood again. "I am Edward Tyrington, and I have a friend whom you might know who was—is—recently deceased. His name is Henri le Marchal."

Bergeron's shoulders relaxed. "Edward Tyrington. From Essex."

"Yes, my father was—"

"I know who your father was, and that your brother is now the earl of Essex. I cannot imagine why you felt the need to come here under false pretenses." He returned to the spirits table, poured two glasses, and handed one to Edward. "You are doing something at Notre Dame, are you not?"

"Yes. There are Roman ruins next to the cathedral, and we are excavating them. I am an archaeologist."

"Fascinating. I am a collector of antiquities, among other things."

"Such as furniture?"

Bergeron went to stoke the fire. "You have a keen eye. However, it is not just furniture. I appreciate...useful art. The artisans of the world who make exceptional everyday goods, those who can take a familiar and useful form and add something creative and beautiful to it, give it a transcendence above its purpose—those are the pieces I collect."

"I see that in the furnishings you have chosen. How do you know so much about me? I thought I was keeping a rather low profile."

"It is my business to know who is about. So what is your interest in elephants, or was that a ruse as well?"

Edward took a sip of whiskey. It was old and smooth, and the smoky flavor was such a pleasure he hated to open his mouth to answer.

"Personally, I have no particular interest in elephants, but I found several manifests from your ships in Henri le Marchal's apartment that reference shipping elephants, and I was wondering why he would have your manifests."

"May I see them?"

Edward removed one receipt that listed elephants from his pocket and handed it to him.

Bergeron stood and paced the room, and at length turned to face Edward. "How well do you know Henri?"

"Quite well."

"And how well do you know Catherine Briggs?"

Edward leaned back and leisurely sipped his drink. Bergeron was already steering the conversation into dangerous territory, and Edward did his best to deflect this tack by calmly saying, "I see no need to bring her into this conversation."

"I believe she was the one who arranged this appointment, despite her best efforts to conceal that it was she making the request." He walked to his humidor, pulled a cigar, and lit it. Between puffs he said, "Or did you think I did not know?"

Edward noted and dismissed the lack of hospitality in Bergeron's failure to offer him a cigar. Considering the lie he made the appointment with, that seemed the least offensive slight he might have endured. Despite Edward's hesitancy regarding the subject of his appointment, he tried to make light of it.

"Apparently you knew of her involvement before even I did. So what of it?"

Bergeron stood before Edward. "Nothing. Except she seems quite involved with your friend Henri."

Edward finished his drink. "Your focus on Miss Briggs is misplaced."

Bergeron stood. "Come with me."

He led Edward through a large glittering ballroom with gold-topped columns and gold drapery swags that offset the deepest azure-blue walls. Their footsteps echoed on the gleaming white marble floor. A door stood on the far side of the room and a flight of steps that swept to the right as they descended to a hall on a lower level. Down the hall, they came to a large door, several times the size of a normal door.

Bergeron stopped. "I demand secrecy regarding what I am about to show you. Do you agree?"

Edward remembered Catherine's fear about Bergeron. "Yes. What does this have to do with Henri?"

"Perhaps nothing, perhaps everything. It will be up to you to find out." He pushed open the door to reveal a truly spectacular room, at least twenty-five feet in either direction and two stories tall, with large windows in two of the walls. White draperies covered the lower ten feet of the windows, which prevented anyone outside from viewing the interior of the room. The upper ten feet of window showed a beautiful view of the treetops at the edge of garden and the sky beyond. Bright green carpeting that looked remarkably like grass covered the floor, and the ceiling resembled a deep-blue firmament, with soft white clouds skittering across its domed surface. There were red velvet sofas and fainting couches along the walls with small tables, but no other furniture.

The centerpiece of the room was a tribe of eight life-size elephant sculptures. Each wore a leather headdress of red flowers in a pattern of golden curves over a black background. Despite the fine pattern, the surface looked rough. The armor over their backs had the same red floral pattern with gold. The tassels hanging at the edges appeared to be made of pure gold and looked as if they could fly in a breeze, they were so delicate. Each had black bracelets with the same swirling gold pattern on each ankle. Their tusks were ivory, pitted and rough with battle, and their eyes were pure, smooth onyx. Edward saw his own distorted reflection in the elephant's eye, the majesty of the animal making a mockery of his gawking. Each ear was gently curved, some smooth, some nicked, and their trunks were raised high. Edward could almost hear their trumpeting. Bergeron walked around the room, lighting lamps between each window frame. The warm yellow light grew more intense as he went. Bergeron asked, "Do you know the provenance of these elephants?"

Edward's mouth had gone dry at the sight of the elephants, and his tongue felt too thick to speak, so he simply shook his head in response.

Bergeron brought him to the closest one and pointed to the head shield on the elephant. "Rajendra. Does that name mean anything?"

Edward cleared his throat and swallowed hard. "I believe he was an Indian ruler."

"Very good, yes. But not just a ruler—the name was also bestowed upon the leader of these elephants."

Edward's incredulous expression questioned Bergeron's statement.

"You still do not know." Bergeron threw his hands in the air and let them fall back to rest on his hips. "Let me enlighten you. What happened to Alexander the Great when he invaded India?"

"He defeated an immense area between Macedonia and India. I believe his last battle was the Battle of Hydaspes. He defeated King Porus, although barely, and kept him as ruler of the area after Porus swore fealty to Alexander. After that Alexander returned home when his troops refused to fight the Nanda Empire further east because the Battle of Hydaspes was so brutal."

"What made that battle so brutal?"

Edward's eyes grew wide. "Elephants."

CHAPTER NINE

B ergeron gestured across the room. "These elephants, to be exact. After Alexander returned home and left King Porus in charge, the king secretly had statues made of each of the elephants that fought against Alexander's forces and ended his march across the subcontinent. There were originally one hundred elephant statues, but only twelve survive today. Eight are here in this room, and someone stole the four others from me."

Edward moved closer to Rajendra and lifted his hand above the scarred trunk. "May I?"

Bergeron nodded, and Edward stroked the elephant's trunk. The gray marble was cold and smooth except for the details of each line, each wrinkle, each cut. He moved his hand to the animal's shoulder. Edward could feel every muscle, some tensed, some at rest, as it stood. The detail was fantastic, and it transported him to a time when these beasts were worshipped for saving a region from a marauding foreign army. He walked all the way around the elephant. The detail in the battle armor was unprecedented. Each nick and scar was faithfully preserved by the artisan. The saddle had gold stars on an azure-blue field with gold edging and tassels along the bottom. Each strap was black leather, some with cracks from age.

He turned to Bergeron. "These are incredible. How did you come to possess them?"

"All that matters is that I possess them. Do you believe they would be better off in a museum?"

Edward scanned the room again. It was an incredible space designed to show the elephants' glory without distraction. "The home you have made for them is unparalleled, but the point of a museum is to let the public view them and learn the history associated with them. The public has a right to learn from these artifacts."

"Right? What right? The public is a teeming swarm of unwashed, uncultured vermin. I paid for these. I brought them here. The public has no rights, and you are a fool to believe they do."

Edward turned to inspect the next elephant. "Regardless of what I think of your black-market purchase, what do these elephants have to do with Henri?"

"Perhaps he went searching for the remaining four."

"You sent him to Nancy. Did he make any contacts there? Any enemies?"

Bergeron walked to the window, pushed back the curtain, and watched as the long shadows of afternoon stalked across the rolling hills of his estate. Through the window Edward saw Bergeron's staff light torches in the garden outside, with its stately arbors and Greek statuary, no doubt stolen from several excavations. It rankled Edward to be in the presence of this man. To see the black-market items, his rank and privilege allowed him to steal and buy unfettered by the law and hindered only by a price he was so willing and able to pay. It jarred him back to reality when Bergeron spoke again after several minutes of silence.

"I told Henri the story of how I had paid for the four elephants and how I had shipped them from India each on a different boat so that if a ship sank, the remaining elephants would be safe. I took every precaution, but I did not bargain that a rival black marketeer would steal the elephants from two of my warehouses."

"Stole them? How? They must weigh thousands of pounds each."

Bergeron returned to Edward, next to the elephants. "They were waiting for transfer to be brought here. There is ample equipment in the warehouse to manage such things."

"Was the thief someone in the warehouse?"

"That is what Henri was going to find out. Understanding, of course, that a finder's fee for such precious objects would be more than worth his time."

Finally, Edward was getting some useful information. "You sent him to recover them. Excellent. Had he contacted your employees? Or the other black marketeer?"

Bergeron smiled. "Henri is a very dear friend to you, is he not?"

Edward straightened and tried to smile, but Bergeron's demeanor, his slick smile, and his tunneling gaze set off warnings in his head. "Given how much you seem to know about me, you already know the answer to that."

"Of course." Bergeron clasped his hands together. "And in return for information on your precious thing, I would like a precious thing from you."

Edward pretended to examine the elephant's armor. "Go on."

"You are betrothed to Catherine Briggs."

Edward turned. His eyes bored into Bergeron's. "Leave her out of this."

Bergeron gave a greasy smile that was more reptilian than human. "Unlikely. Your future father-in-law is my biggest competitor, and he has something I want."

Edward turned back toward another elephant, named Ahibaran based on the engraving on the saddle, and studied its saddle. "Then ask him for it."

Bergeron gave a great belly laugh, as if Edward had told the funniest joke of the year. When he caught his breath, he said, "In our business, we have certain secrets. For instance, I sell a particular type of silk from a particular region in China that is unmatched for its softness and the fastness of its color. I found the artisans and have made it worth their while to only trade through me, and to keep their art secret so another dealer cannot court them. Briggs has a glassblower. I believe he is in Italy, but I am uncertain where in Italy. Briggs has struck the same type of deal with him. He, or they, work in secret. No one knows who produces glass with such lightness, clarity, or beauty. But you are going to find out. And you are going to tell me."

"How do you expect me to do that? I have no interest in shipping, nor do I understand a thing about glass blowing."

"But as his future son-in-law, you will need to learn these things. Besides, it is a poorly kept secret that your betrothed is the person managing the business and has been for some time now. Perhaps love will loosen her tongue."

Edward clenched his teeth. This extortion over Henri was galling, and he knew Bergeron would never believe that his betrothal was a ruse. "How can you live with yourself knowing that a man's killer may walk free and you refuse to help bring him justice by demanding an impossible payment?"

Bergeron walked toward the door. "Perhaps you are the wrong man for this proposition. You are brash and easily defeated. And young for such an endeavor. Although I knew Henri could manage it, I hold no such esteem for your abilities."

Edward stood firm and crossed his arms, saying nothing.

"I will tell you he contacted several people at the warehouse in Nancy, including my foreman Mr. Latour, but further information regarding his other contacts will depend on your success in obtaining the secret I desire or finding my elephants." Bergeron went to the door of the study and extended a hand, indicating to Edward it was time for him to leave.

The ride home seemed interminable. *How will I possibly get this information from Catherine? If I do, she will never forgive me.* His heart felt heavy at the thought of betraying her. Would it be worth it if Bergeron had information about Henri's murderer? Edward chastised himself.

The night had turned chilly, and he felt exhausted, dizzy even. As the carriage jostled and bounced the way home, Edward held the doorhandle but still had difficulty with all the movement. He did not recall the ride to Bergeron's being so unsettling, but he put it out of his mind as a case of nerves. It had been an extremely trying day.

CHAPTER TEN

I t was a testament to Davis's efficiency. He had packed Edward's bags, and the two men arrived at the station at half-past five. When Edward hired a carriage to take them to the train station, Davis had the temerity to ask to ride in the coach with Edward "to discuss the logistics of the trip." Edward overlooked the breach of protocol, knowing that for Davis to do so meant something was afoot.

Davis sat across from Edward, and as the carriage pulled from the curb, he fiddled with the deep green curtains and remarked on the plushness of the seats. Finally Edward said, "It seems incredible that you asked to ride in the carriage with me to remark on the seats."

Davis stopped fidgeting. "No, sir. I do not wish to take liberties, but your father would not want me to hold my tongue about the impropriety of you traveling with a woman who is not your wife. You should consider the damage this trip may do to her reputation, and yours. There will be talk about this. Think of how that talk might affect poor Charles."

Edward refrained from rolling his eyes only because of the esteem he had for Davis and the many times he had helped him in difficult situations. He could not hold his tongue about the comment on Charles, though. "Poor Charles? Lord Tyrington? *That* poor Charles? I can assure you he has far more pressing concerns than his brother's traveling companion. Besides, Miss Briggs has arranged for a chaperone. And we also have you and Miss Daniella. You remember her lady's maid, I assume."

Davis's lips thinned. "It is inappropriate that *you* should know the name of her lady's maid."

Edward lit his pipe. "Please, Davis, this trip will go far more smoothly if you let go of a bit of the eighteenth-century rigidity. Let us simply focus on our task."

Davis looked less than comforted as the carriage stopped and they disembarked. A cool breeze blew, and Edward pulled his collar tight against his neck. The station was a swarm of people, some arriving, some departing, some intent on moving as quickly as possible, others walking as if they had decades to reach their destination. The slow people annoyed Edward, and he passed them in haste, willing them to move to the platform's edge to allow him to proceed unhindered. But of course, those who walked slowly did not care one whit what he thought, and it rankled him. His nerves about this trip had him feeling more sensitive than usual, and he willed himself to trust that somehow he would bring justice for Henri's murder. He forced himself to slow down after he and Davis passed several groups of people. They finally found Catherine with her lady's maid in tow at the platform, and they made introductions. Davis and Miss Daniella left for the third-class carriage.

Edward said, "I was under the impression you had arranged for a chaperone for this trip?"

Catherine looked around nervously, standing on her tiptoes to see over the crowd. "My uncle will join us. He should be here already. He is a large man with gray hair. Please help me look for him. It is almost time to board."

Edward looked over Catherine's shoulder and turned anti-clockwise to search the crowd. He had almost made a full circle when he heard a voice behind.

"Hello Catherine, darling, how are you? So wonderful to see you again."

Edward turned and saw a man significantly shorter than him, the top of his hat being below Edward's jaw. His face was jovial with a bright smile, but a large, bulbous, red nose marred it. His clothing was of the latest fashion, with a loose waistcoat in a doeskin color that hid his portly midsection, plus a black bowtie and shoes. If he were slimmer and younger, he could have stood in as a model for the House of Worth. He was easily the most fashionably dressed man Edward had seen in a while, and in Paris, that was surprising.

He kissed Catherine's hand as she introduced them. "Mr. Tyrington, this is my uncle, Hieronymus Willoughby."

Edward shook his hand. "Edward Tyrington. Pleasure to meet you."

"Please call me Hero. Far less pretentious than Hieronymus."

Edward cocked his head and smiled in confusion. Hero chuckled, and his meaty hand shook Edward's longer than dictated by decorum. Edward finally pulled back and tucked his hand in his pocket as the exchange slipped from congenial to uncomfortable.

Catherine nervously smiled. "Shall we find our coach, then?" Hero offered his arm to her, and Edward followed toward the front of the train.

They entered their private coach. It was about twelve feet long with rosewood wainscoting and red velvet wallpaper above. A large oriental rug covered the floor. There were two love seats, two cushioned chairs situated around a low table, and two additional chairs on either side of a writing table. There were banks of windows along either side, with heavy claret curtains tied between each window. Beams of rosewood outlined the coffered ceiling with whitewashed panels between.

Edward chose a chair by the window and watched the crowd hurry onto the train as the whistle blew, signaling imminent departure. Hero settled on a sofa, while Catherine chose a chair at the writing table. She removed her tatting shuttle from her bag and swiftly wound it through the string in a series of moves that left Edward sure he could never do such a thing in his life.

"What are you making?"

"A pair of lace gloves. I have only just started."

Hero interjected, "My niece is quite handy, Mr. Tyrington. I have filled my home with her beautiful works of lace and needlepoint."

Edward's stomach churned at the thought of yet another man trying to sell Catherine as marriageable goods, and he responded with a halfhearted, "I am sure, but please call me Edward." As the train slowly rumbled from the station and gathered speed, he asked, "Where do you live, Hero?"

"South of the small town of Chinon in the Loire Valley. My vineyard produces Cabernet Franc. Have you tried Bouchet Cabernet?"

"I confess I have not."

"Ah, we will have to rectify that." He retrieved his small bag and brought it to the table. He removed a bottle of wine, a decanter, and three small silver cups. "I never travel without a bottle or two. My grapes are the finest black grapes of the region." He uncorked and decanted the bottle, and after a few minutes, he poured and passed cups to Edward and Catherine. "À votre santé."

"À la tienne!"

Edward swirled the wine and smelled a light peppery scent. The wine was a lighter red than he was used to but quite enjoyable. "This is lovely." He sipped again. "There is a slight floral finish. What is that?"

Hero beamed. "You have a good nose. That is my vineyard's secret."

The word *secret* startled Edward as he remembered his mission to extract information from Catherine.

Hero spoke more of wine and wineries, his vintner friend whom they planned to visit upon their arrival, and his wonderful Gris de Toul Gamay wine. Edward did not know there were so many words to describe a wine, but Hero certainly did. After several exhaustive descriptions of wines and vines, Hero finally settled on palace gossip. Edward lost interest early on and paid little attention, grunting to show agreement here and there as he watched the sun set behind the fiery autumn countryside. The dark, muscular tree trunks were slick from a recent rain, contrasting with the brilliant reds, oranges, and yellows of the wet leaves glinting as they raced past. He imagined them dancing, as if the entire forest had joined a bawdy maypole celebration while he sat in the stifling coach. He caught Catherine's eye once, and she smiled as Hero continued to prattle on.

Hero poured more wine for himself and Edward refused, having sipped his more slowly. It dawned on Edward that perhaps he knew who the glassblower that Bergeron sought was. Edward carefully steered the conversation from wine making to wine distribution. Catherine interjected some points about the lengths of time to ship from one region to another. Edward was sure to keep the conversation light but relevant enough that he could refer to it when he and Hero were alone in order to pursue his goal. When Hero opened the second bottle of wine, Edward suggested he and Hero retire to the smoking lounge for a cigar.

Hero took up his bottle. "That sounds lovely. You will be all right on your own for a while, Catherine?" Before she could answer or Edward could even stand, Hero was marching toward the door, full glass in his right hand and a bottle tucked in his left elbow. His feet purposefully counterbalanced the sway of the train and the sway of the wine as best he could.

Catherine gripped Edward's arm. "It would be prudent to discourage his drinking."

Edward nodded and hurried after Hero, having no intention of discouraging him.

The smoking car was plush with deep-blue wingback chairs, small oak tables, and ashtray stands near each. The crowded room made Edward wonder if the men had simply skipped the first-class car and boarded directly here. Hero had already selected a table and was pouring his next glass of wine. Edward joined him.

As Hero filled his glass, he said, "So nice to be away from my niece's baleful glare. She will make a wonderful wife for you Edward, but you must realize she is a bit of a teetotaler."

Edward decided finding common ground with Hero was of the utmost importance. "Yes, well, all women are, I suppose. At least the ones worthy of marriage."

Hero laughed and smacked him on the back. "I suppose that's why I have never married!"

Edward raised his glass. "Let us drink to that." After Hero had another sip, Edward said, "What are your thoughts on home decoration? I am considering some improvements to my home in Paris."

Edward smoked a cigar while Hero derided the misguided overwrought nature of Rococo and Gothic Revival and praised an up-and-coming designer named Eastlake who used simpler lines and more straight forward ornamentation that was more to his own taste. It astonished Edward how long Hero could prattle on with minimal input from Edward. A few well-placed "mm-hmms" and Hero carried all the conversation.

After they finished the first bottle of wine, Edward homed in on his mark. "What about glass? I have a chandelier that I would like to change the globes."

"Ah, if you want the finest glass, speak to my brother. He imports the best quality glass there is."

"From where?"

"Italy."

"Anywhere special in Italy? Or is the entire country rife with talented glass blowers?"

"I do not know specifics, other than the group in question works by the sea. I recall hearing a story about them and the sea, but I do not remember the details. There was an old man and a group of young men who help him. Perhaps he is even dead now. It has been years since we discussed it. You should ask Catherine."

"Oh, no, I would rather surprise her with them. I will ask John when we return. Please do not mention my inquiry to her."

Hero smiled. "Of course."

Edward gathered up the glasses. "We should probably return to Catherine. I expect we will arrive in Nancy within the hour."

CHAPTER ELEVEN

When the train stopped at their station, they disembarked in darkness. The station signs were still dripping, but the rain had stopped for now. Hero jumped up and left for Monsieur Roche's vineyard as soon as the train stopped, saying his man would bring his bags to the inn.

Edward stepped out of the train. The brisk air felt wonderful, and he breathed deeply. He took Catherine's hand and helped her down the stairs. Edward felt a bit wobbly after the fast-moving train ride, and for a moment he swayed as the scene before him melted and swam before his eyes. He thought perhaps the alcohol was too much for him.

Catherine dropped her tatting bag, and her left hand shot up to his forehead. "You are feverish." She turned toward the back of the train and yelled. "Davis! Davis!"

Davis came running. "Here, ma'am."

"He has a fever."

Did Edward imagine it, or had the crowd on the platform that swarmed past them moved further away?

Davis put his hand to Edward's forehead. Edward stumbled back slightly but caught himself. "I am fine. It was stuffy in the coach."

"Nonsense. Miss Briggs, it will be faster if you can you take him in the carriage while Miss Daniella and I manage the bags. When you arrive at the inn, put cold compresses on his head. I will be along as quickly as possible."

"Of course." She took Edward by the arm as Davis hurried back to the luggage compartment. Edward protested as best he could, but she would hear none of it.

Edward gazed out the window as they drove to the inn. The brilliance of autumn was diminished here, and everything seemed to whisper of death. There were more leaves on the ground, with carpets of red and brown along the roadway woven with puddles reflecting the gaslights as they passed. Soon they were driving past buildings that grew in size as they approached the center of town.

The inn was a four-story brick building. Catherine helped him to a chair in the lobby and checked them in, claiming he was motion sick from the train, then guided him to his room. He stumbled on the stairs, and Catherine caught him. Beads of sweat soaked his entire body, as if his skin had released an ocean. She held him up as she unlocked the door. Once inside, he fell into bed. He felt a cold compress on his head and felt his shoes slip off, then all was darkness.

He awoke with Catherine bending over him. She smiled at seeing him awake and gazed into his eyes. He saw her breath quicken slightly, with goosebumps rising on her skin. She removed the compress from his head, kissed his forehead, and put the compress back. His shirt was off, and she rinsed and replaced the compresses on his chest. They felt cool against his skin, as a few drops of water trickled down to his belly and down his sides. She lifted his head and helped him drink water. The water he sipped had an odd taste, somewhat warm and earthy, but also crisp, and he pulled back from it for a moment.

"Tincture of Willow," Catherine said as she helped him sip more, "for your fever."

After he drank, she returned his head to the feather pillow and softly stroked his hand. He barely breathed, afraid to break the spell as he slipped deep into the blue pools of her eyes, drowning in them as he had always wanted to do—but not in a frightened, struggling way, rather in a way that felt like he was finally home.

Sometime later, he awoke drenched in sweat as a fire roared beside him in the grate. Davis came to the edge of his bed from a dark corner of the room.

"If you are able, sir, you should have some bone broth."

Edward nodded his head, which set off a flurry of fireworks behind his eyes. He covered his eyes and rubbed his head to stop the searing pain. "There is a stabbing pain in my head."

"You have a fever, sir. Here, drink this." Davis spooned some broth into his mouth. It had a rich flavor of beef and an earthiness of mushrooms. He ate several bites, then laid back down to rest. Sitting up was excruciating. He rolled over and watched the fire for a while and then must have fallen asleep.

He dreamed he was back in Egypt with Henri. Their work at the Suez Canal was just beginning, but he and Henri had to oversee the workers digging the canal. As the workers dug and chanted songs to keep time, a steam shovel operator lost control. The shovel crushed dozens of people, including Henri. Edward screamed in his dream and awoke with a start. Catherine came from the shadows as he sat bolt upright. Had he cried out? He was not sure, but he thought so.

Catherine said, "It was only a dream. You are all right now."

He sighed and tried to calm his heart, but the image of the steam shovel careening toward the workers haunted him. His throat burned, as did his head, and every joint in his body felt achy and stiff.

Catherine helped him sip more water. He asked her to tell him a story since he could barely speak.

"I will tell you of one of my favorite memories."

Edward half-smiled and watched her eyes sparkle in the firelight.

"I was seventeen, and my father took me to a series of five towns in the Kingdom of Lombardy. Each town is in a bowl between the mountains and the sea, and is built almost as if it were hanging from the cliffs. The buildings are all painted in bright reds, blues, and yellows leading to the water. My father decided we should hike the mountains between the towns and stay in each town for several weeks. It would take a good part of a day to hike from one town to the next. The views from up high in the mountains overlooking the crystal-blue water were stunning. It was there I met Giuseppe. He worked in a hotel in the town of Riomaggiore. Our rooms there overlooked the water, where the sunsets were spectacular. Giuseppe was about my age and, despite the language barrier, we communicated well. Sometimes I would sneak away while my father worked, and we would walk off to the cliffs over the sea or through the vineyards on the steep mountain slopes. Giuseppe brought me pastries from the bakery that were still hot from the oven. Torrone, sfogliatella, cannoli, they were all so delicious. It was only a few days that we stayed there, but I sometimes wonder where Giuseppe is today."

Edward smiled as he imagined a young Catherine eating pastries with a boy who did not share her language. It would be scandalous in Britain, but in the wilds of northern Italy, he supposed anything was possible. In the warm room with such happy thoughts, and seeing the wistful smile on Catherine's face, his eyelids fluttered heavily and fell into a deep sleep.

At some point, he dreamed of Charles, who was fretting. Typical Charles. For the child who held the title of Lord Tyrington, he seemed to have no composure. In Edward's dream Charles's entire head was shaking, from the top of his dark, close-cropped hair with its receding hairline all the way to his jowls, which gave him a rather bulldog appearance, so unlike Edward and Thaddeus. Edward wondered why on earth he was so upset and surmised it must have been Thaddeus, whose face swam in and out of view, only as solid as the scent of a cigar after someone has left the room. A hint, a vapor, nothing more. It was as if he was playing hide and seek, and no one could find him. Edward had looked, and Charles had reacted poorly when Edward could not find him, but neither could Charles. As his anger rose, his head shook more violently.

Edward awoke briefly with Davis by his bedside. He looked old and worn, his clothing more disheveled than Edward had ever seen him, with buttons missing and his collar unpinned. Davis's mouth moved, but he heard no sound. Davis showed him a glass of water, and Edward looked away. The windows were dark. There was a roaring fire, then nothing more but blackness and heat.

CHAPTER TWELVE

E dward awoke in the morning—he thought. At least there was sun coming through the windows. Catherine was asleep in the chair by his bed with sunlight gleaming off her strawberry-blond hair. He remembered her placing compresses on his chest, and his heart swelled. He watched her sleep and knew he would forsake every other woman for her. She was the only one who truly understood him, even in ways he barely understood himself. *You are not worthy of her, Edward. You are everything your father said you were, and worse.* He gave a small sigh, thinking of his inadequacy and the pain it had caused him his whole life.

She exhaled softly as her eyes fluttered open. He was staring at her as she leaned forward. "Are you awake? Can you speak?"

"Of course I can."

She jumped up and grabbed his hands. "Thank God! Davis!" she shouted. "He is awake!"

Davis came running in and saw him. "You gave us quite a scare, sir." He felt Edward's head for fever and checked his pulse.

Catherine smiled. "You have been delirious with fever for three days."

Edward tried to sit up, but the room spun and he melted back down into his pillow. "Apparently."

Davis put his hand on Edward's chest. "Miss Briggs, may I have a few moments to examine the patient?" When she left, he said, "You have had a terrible illness. Dire enough that I wired Charles out of concern that you might die. He was going to leave Essex tonight if you did not improve. I will send a wire that you are better, unless you would like him to come here."

"Definitely not. The last thing I need is Charles's interference. However, I would like a rasher of bacon and some eggs. I am starving."

"You should have bone broth and a day of rest."

"I appreciate your care, but I have lost three days of investigation. When is Davet's funeral?"

"In about three hours, sir."

"Excellent, we shall start there."

The afternoon was bright, and the temperature had dropped over the intervening days to be colder than normal. Edward alighted from the carriage and held out a hand for Catherine. Her pursed lips and furrowed brow scrawled concern on her face. She had argued with him about whether he should come to the funeral, which she had planned to attend with Hero, and wanted to make sure Edward did not have a relapse. He tried to get her to have the discussion quietly in his room, but she raised her voice. Ultimately, he informed her that he was attending with or without her and Davis, so they both might as well accept the fact. He spoke to Hero before entering the carriage, and Hero agreed to assist him in any way possible that was not doting over his health. He understood that sometimes a man simply needed to take action.

Davet's funeral mass was at St. Sebastian in the center of town. The church rose above the surrounding plaza in white marble with friezes carved on either side of the main door. Above this entrance was a large window with a statue of St. Peter on one side and St. Sebastien on the other, and a clock tower rising above. It appeared as if the whole town had turned out to celebrate Davet's life and mourn his death. Although Edward knew that many of those in attendance were probably relatives, he noticed a group of university types, with a few older men and at least a dozen college-age young men, who were probably colleagues of Davet's. Catherine greeted a woman nearby who turned out to be a second cousin of Henri's. The chatter amongst those milling about outside was mostly in hushed tones regarding the shocking nature of the murders. Edward greeted the woman when Catherine introduced her, then he scanned the crowd for anything out of the ordinary. Since he did not know most of the people, it was hard to tell just what was out of the ordinary, but he kept his eyes open. As Catherine was wrapping up her conversation, Edward asked if the woman could point out Evaline so they could pay their respects.

"Have you not heard? Evaline disappeared the night they killed her husband."

Catherine's jaw dropped. "What? No one mentioned this."

The woman's voice became quiet. "Yes, the police think she may be a suspect. Although anyone who knows her knows that could not possibly be right. Something happened to her. I only wish they knew what. She was such a dear; she never could have hurt Davet and Henri."

Catherine mumbled the words "Thank you" and walked away. Edward followed her.

"Are you all right?" he asked. "Do you need to sit down?"

"What does this mean, Edward? I agree that her being the murderer is unlikely, but where is she?"

"Is there someone else here who might know more about it?"

Hero walked up as Catherine scanned the crowd. "Did you hear Evaline is missing?"

Edward answered. "We just heard. Who else is here that might know more about what happened?"

Hero held his hands up and slowly lowered them as he spoke. "Now is not the time, Edward. We should ask Davet's mother, but later, not now."

Edward agreed, and they filed into the church for the service. Entering the vestibule, Edward smelled the traditional Catholic incense. He recalled Henri referring to church as "smells and bells" and smirked. He passed the vessel of holy water at the entrance and saw the others dousing a finger and making the sign of the cross with it. Being an irreligious Anglican, Edward passed by without blessing himself. There were four large windows that spanned several stories on either side of the dark mahogany pews. Three steps the width of the nave led up to the altar, which stood empty now, awaiting the priest. Davet's mother sat in the front row, dressed in black, with a black veil covering her head. Next to her sat a man—Edward was not sure who he was since Davet's father had died years before—and other family filled out the remaining front two rows. He and his companions sat near the back of the church to have a clear view of most of the people there, even if they were viewing the attendees' backs.

The choir, seated in the loft above, began singing with an organ accompaniment. The soprano voices of the boys gave a lofty air to the hymn "In Paradisum." It was only in this moment, as the crowd hushed and took their seats with the Latin refrain ringing through the church, that Edward stopped focusing on the investigation and remembered that above all, this was a funeral. He felt cheated that he had not attended Henri's funeral, and for what? He had wasted two days with a fever, and likely the trail of any investigation was already cold.

The priest spoke about the loss of Davet and the horrible crime committed in their community. Edward watched the crowd for any unusual reactions to his words. One woman seemed to weep harder than most. She had dark hair pulled into a tight bun with a small black veil pinned into it. Edward nudged Catherine with his elbow and nodded in the woman's direction.

Catherine leaned in and whispered, "Maria."

So that was the Maria Henri had spoken of. "Why is she not in Paris?"

"They did not invite her. Only close family knew when the funeral was."

A woman behind them leaned forward and shushed them, and Edward went back to observing the crowd.

The priest spoke of Davet's contribution to the community, his work as a professor, and then focused on who he truly was: a good man. Good to his neighbors, good to his family, good to his wife, and good to strangers in need. Edward wondered what the priest had said about Henri. Surely he knew their family and had known Henri as a child, but he did not know the Henri that Edward knew. Although Henri was forced to attend church as a condition of their return from exile, Edward knew he had sat at the back, away from his family, and daydreamed the entire time. He wondered if the priest's condemnation of Henri's irreligious nature was evident in his eulogy and assumed it likely was. *To hell with that priest.*

The longer the priest spoke about Davet, the more prevalent Edward's sorrow became until finally he broke down in tears. Although he did not know Davet, he saw the impact he had had on his community, the words of good deeds recounted by the priest, the tears and sobs from family and friends, the number of people in attendance that left no seat empty and half the walls at the back of the church lined with people standing. Henri's father had ensured his funeral would be small. Edward could not fathom how a father would want to limit the mourning of his son and wondered if there was a reason. Did Alfonse know more about what happened to Henri than even Madame le Marchal knew? That thought stopped his tears for a few moments as he reviewed what little he knew.

He surreptitiously looked around the church again. There were very few who were not crying. He estimated there were two hundred people there. Edward could count the people who knew or cared for him on one hand. Surely there would be others at his own funeral. His brother Charles, Lord Tyrington, would not be above using Edward's funeral as political goodwill if Edward predeceased him, which only compounded his sadness. Of the few who might attend his funeral, only a handful would know him at all.

After the funeral, they exited the church into the sunny afternoon, which felt warm and inviting, though the areas in shade were ice cold. Catherine rubbed her arms, and they walked to their carriage.

As Edward opened the door, a woman across the square screamed, "How dare you!"

Everyone's head turned toward two women facing each other on the church steps. One was taller and more slender than the other, but in their black veils, it was hard to make out anything else about them. The taller one tried to walk away, but the other woman grabbed her arm.

The taller woman yelled, "Leave me alone! I am here to pay my respects, same as you."

The shorter woman kept trying to grab at her or hit her. It was hard to tell. "Your sister disappeared after the murder," she said. "I bet she had a hand in it. Your whole family is trouble."

A group of men separated the women, and Edward sneaked a glance at Catherine, who said, "Evaline's second cousin, Chloe Bellon."

"Who is the yelling woman?"

"I believe a cousin of Davet's. Perhaps Matilde. It is difficult to see with her veil. She was close to Davet when they were children, which might explain her reaction."

"Why does she think Evaline's family is trouble? Is there a history there?"

Catherine shrugged. "I do not know, but Chloe is the only one here from Evaline's side of the family, which is quite unusual. I can say that Evaline had nothing to do with this. They were devoted to each other."

The scuffle continued while Matilde's family kept her at bay, until Chloe entered a waiting carriage driven by one of the university students and sped off.

"Should we speak to Matilde?"

Hero stepped in front of Edward. "Again, Edward, now is not the time. What you should do is rest."

Catherine turned to stand shoulder to shoulder with Hero. "I quite agree. Nothing is to be gained by intruding on everyone's grief."

Rather than fight an uphill battle to continue their investigation that day, he relented. "Fine. We will begin in the morning."

CHAPTER THIRTEEN

E dward awoke the next morning as the sun broke, casting brilliant shafts of light onto the blond teak wooden bedposts in his room. As several boats floated slowly by outside his window—some under steam power, others under sails—and the butchers and vegetable sellers set up on the square, he felt a moment of peace. A deep abiding peace. Like being comforted by his mother, as if there was some assurance that everything would somehow be all right. He let himself bask in peacefulness as he watched the children of the fish mongers play jacks and knucklebones by the quay or run past with their rolling hoops. He sat at the desk to make a list of people to interview and questions to ask.

The hotel had a restaurant and at breakfast, Hero announced he would visit another vineyard and would likely not be returning until the next morning. Apparently, a nearby vineyard requested his expertise on the grape blight. Edward wondered why Hero had agreed to chaperone Catherine and himself if he had no intention of spending any time with them at all, but he held his tongue. He would let Catherine handle her uncle and her expectations of him. Perhaps he had only agreed so he could visit wineries across the country.

Edward hired a carriage to go to Bergeron's warehouse. Twenty minutes later, he arrived at a large building on the river with a long brick wall that blocked the view of any activity on the property, and a large wrought-iron gate outside the main entrance that had an imposing effect. At the far end of the wall, Edward noticed a rail line that exited the property. He paid the driver to wait for him.

The office was a sea of calm, with mahogany wood paneling that gave the office an air of professionalism, high quality, and wealth. The ceiling was coffered, with small inlays of African animals in teak, red oak, and gold. Conversations at the various desks were hushed, and Edward assumed Bergeron demanded that all his offices operate in this manner. The far wall held a giant portrait of Gaston Bergeron, looking down over his minions. *Bergeron certainly likes to make his presence felt.*

Edward asked the person at the reception desk to speak to a manager. The man insisted he could help without a manager's involvement until Edward leaned over the counter and whispered, "Monsieur Bergeron requested I see you regarding a special elephant shipment from India."

The clerk said, "Oh, of course. One moment, sir," and hurried off. He returned with another gentleman, who stood a few inches taller than Edward and was twice as wide. The man tilted his head and squinted his eyes. "I was not expecting you until nightfall, but your goods are here. Do you have a carriage that we can load it into?"

Rather than express the confusion he felt, Edward said, "Thank you. Yes, but I would like to inspect the item first."

They entered a hallway that led to a warehouse. As they walked, Edward chastised himself. *What are you thinking? What are you doing?* He had no answer for either question, no matter how many times he posed the questions. His heart pounded faster, knowing that he was on an unknown trajectory with an uncertain end.

They exited the building, and the sunlight was blinding. He blinked several times to help his eyes adjust, and the noise of the shipping yard overtook his internal deliberations. He watched as men ran hither and yon, some transporting crates, others shouting directions to the crews unloading the ships. Large draft horses pulled carts of cargo around the yard. Everything seemed chaotic, and he realized the serene facade of the office was just that, a facade. The operation was just as hectic as Catherine's office, and that gave him some comfort that perhaps Bergeron's operation was not so much more polished and efficient than hers.

They stopped in a distant corner of the yard, and his companion opened a crate with a crowbar then turned his back to give Edward privacy. Edward removed the lid of the crate, and a generous amount of cotton wadding fell out to reveal a jade elephant with ivory tusks. Edward knelt down and pulled the rest of the wadding from around it. The elephant had onyx eyes, and the tusks had gold bands where they met the elephant's face. The pure green jade showed every wrinkle. It had a black saddle, likely carved from onyx. The elephant was the size of a small dog, a hound perhaps, and from his limited view, it seemed perfect in every detail.

Edward stuffed the wadding back into the crate and closed the lid. "Monsieur Bergeron will be well pleased. Where should my carriage enter?"

The man pointed to a gate at the far end of the wall, and Edward left to bring the carriage through. The man hefted the crate into the carriage, then Edward sat next to it as he bid them adieu. Once they left the warehouse, he directed the carriage driver to take him back to the center of town.

CHAPTER FOURTEEN

E dward exited the carriage, and he found the crate was heavy as he walked. He entered the lobby of a hotel and sat for a moment to catch his breath. *If anyone tries to follow me, this will slow them down a bit.* The lobby was shabby, with a blue carpet stained brown in pathways to and from the front desk. Another man in the lobby appeared rather drunk, and he eyed Edward, either suspiciously or as a potential friend, Edward could not quite tell. He gathered his crate and left. He wandered in another direction, then stopped at another inn for a brief respite. The weight of the elephant seemed to grow exponentially with each step, and he mopped his brow as he looked around. A lobby boy asked if he wanted a room or to eat in the dining room. Edward refused and slowly gathered up the crate again as the doorman held the door for him. He took a carriage to yet another inn, then finally took a carriage to his own inn. He skirted through the lobby as quickly as possible and went to his room.

Davis was setting the fire and rose to greet him. "What have you there, sir?"

"An elephant. Help me unpack it."

Davis eyed him as he helped him remove the top of the crate. "You look a bit flushed. Are you all right?"

"I admit I am tired and rather hot, but I have carried this box through the city for over an hour." Edward removed the elephant.

"Where did you purchase this? It is lovely."

"I did not purchase it. In fact, I stole it from Bergeron's warehouse." Edward continued to study the statue and ran his fingers along the creases in the legs.

"Stole?"

"Yes. I told them Bergeron had sent me regarding an elephant shipment from India, and they helpfully assumed I came to collect this artifact."

"And you took it?"

"Well, it seemed a good idea, but now I am rather regretting it. Please go to Miss Briggs's room and request that she join me here."

Davis pursed his lips for a moment then left.

By the time he returned with Catherine in tow, Edward had covered the elephant with the crate. He welcomed her and bid them both to sit. Catherine eyed the crate then looked at him quizzically, but she said nothing as she took the large black wingback chair by the fire. He explained the events whereby he came to have possession of the elephant then removed the crate for to her to inspect it.

She stood, ignoring the statue completely, and stared wide-eyed at Edward. "Do you have any idea what this means? He will kill you to regain possession of this."

Edward half-smiled then sobered his expression. "I think you are being a bit dramatic."

Catherine's eyes turned as cold as the iciest blue within them, and she paced across the room, her bed slippers making soft *wic wic wic* noises as she walked. "No, I am not. I told you before that Bergeron is ruthless, and I meant it." She stopped pacing and faced him. "What could possess you to act as if you were to retrieve this statue?"

Edward turned to the fire. He could not face her and admit how he had betrayed her—or rather, had considered betraying her—but for him, even the consideration of Bergeron's proposition was a betrayal, and nothing could wash the stain of that from his heart. The fire seemed to blaze higher and hotter as he spoke, with flames rising into the chimney as if his own self-recrimination fed them.

"Bergeron told me that the only way he would share all that he knew of Henri's investigation was for me to share a secret with him—specifically, the secret of who your glassblower is in Italy. I did not want to betray your trust. This shipment provides leverage over the situation. I can tell him where his precious cargo is in exchange for the information of what he knows about Henri's investigation."

Catherine's brows furrowed, and her lips parted in an expression that was a mix of fear, disbelief, and—did he imagine it?—admiration. Her reaction was almost too brief to read before her countenance closed like a fan and her voice took on an almost businesslike tone.

"Your attempt to maintain my trust will be of no use if you are dead. Are you so abysmally foolish as to blackmail Bergeron?" She took his hands in hers, her brows raised in concern. "I do not know how to make you understand. I am not being dramatic. There are rumors of how he has dealt with people. Please promise me you will be careful about this. Bergeron is a horrible man."

Edward saw the tears that welled briefly in her eyes. "I am open to suggestions. I cannot just return it now. Should we leave today and take it with us?"

Catherine pulled her hands back. "Under no circumstances will I travel with that stolen statue. We need to send the elephant somewhere for safekeeping. That way they cannot simply kill you and take the elephant. Perhaps..." Catherine's eyes took on a faraway look as she fell silent. "Perhaps...yes. Maxwell would keep it safe for me." Edward watched as Catherine shifted from a fearful woman to someone who commanded her domain. Her shoulders straightened, and her eyes glowed with the spark of a plan.

Chapter Fifteen

Edward asked, "Who is Maxwell and why would he keep the elephant safe?"

"The manager of my father's warehouse in Southampton. I trust Maxwell with my life. Or rather, yours. He will keep it safe, he will not open it, and he will not breathe a word of the package's arrival or instructions to anyone. He is the most inscrutable man I know. You must take it at once to Metz." She went to the oak rolltop desk and scribbled notes on two sheets of paper, then placed them in envelopes sealed with wax imprinted with the Briggs crest ring she wore. "Repackage it."

She handed him one envelope, which said "Monsieur Rochelle" with an address in Metz. She attached the other envelope, which simply said "Maxwell Ramsay, Briggs Warehouse, Southampton," to the crate.

"Take the crate to the Monsieur Rochelle and have him read this letter. Await an answer from him before you return. If he asks you anything, you must say that my father instructed you to bring it to him. If he agrees, he will take care of shipping the elephant."

"Your father? But you signed the letter."

"I signed my father's signature, as I do for every transaction in the company. You cannot believe that an entire worldwide shipping organization would take direction from a woman, do you? Please go now."

Edward's heart filled with admiration that she both did so much for her father's company and did it in a way that minimized resistance. He was proud of her, but his words ended up sounding patronizing.

"This seems rather too much. Perhaps we should explain that I had a misunderstanding..."

"It is too late for that. Get rid of this thing today. Go!"

Edward donned his coat, and Davis said, "I am going with you." They took the crate and left.

Davis hired a carriage while Edward held the crate in a darkened stairwell. At Davis's signal, Edward slipped from the shadows and into the coach as quickly as possible. He did not want to ruin all his work to cover his tracks by being spotted now. The crate sat between them like a wall. They spoke no words across it and stared out their respective windows.

Finally, when they were well outside town, Davis dared speak. "If Catherine is correct—"

"Please, Davis, not now. I cannot bear the thought that she may be right and my impulsive decision has brought such danger down on us."

"I was going to say that I will do all I can to protect you, sir."

Edward sighed and ran his fingers through his hair. "I apologize, Davis. I should have never tried such a gambit. But I must know what Bergeron knows and without betraying Miss Briggs's trust."

"Of course."

Edward leaned his head back against the seat and sighed again. There was nothing else to say. His mind filled with regret for his impulsiveness, for his lack of forethought. The words rang in his head in his father's voice, where he had heard them so often when he was young. He recalled his father teaching him and Henri to pick locks and watching Lord Tyrington's obvious admiration of Henri's skills, which far surpassed his own. The tone in his father's voice praising Henri and belittling Edward in the most condescending way possible only hardened his own self-loathing. Henri was the son his own father wished he'd had, because Edward was too impulsive, too forgetful, and too unfit for most tasks set before him.

Outside of town, Edward and Davis stopped at a livery stable and rented another carriage. It looked marginally roadworthy, with worn seat fabric and a bowed driver's seat from the weight of the drivers. The horse seemed sturdy; at least that was something. Davis drove, and since the day was sunny, Edward sat next to him. Edward placed the crate in the carriage compartment under a saddle blanket.

Despite the beauty of the afternoon, Edward was pensive and silent as they rode. Further from town, the road was less traveled and became more rutted. Their progress slowed as they carefully avoided rocks and washouts, but the view was lovely. They passed several farms along the way, some with haybales scattered across the fields.

Despite the afternoon sun, which filtered through the surrounding forest in green and gold, there was a stretch of mud that was barely a single track. Edward remarked that perhaps they had come the wrong way, but there was nowhere to turn around, so they pressed on.

As they came around a bend, a man on a dull brown horse pulled in front of them. He pointed a gun at them, and Edward saw little else of him, other than his hat was low over his face and he wore a long black coat. As this man ordered them off the carriage, another man pulled up his black horse across the path behind them. The man with the gun grabbed the reins of their horse, and the second man demanded their valuables. As Edward handed over his wallet and a silver pocket watch, he hoped they would not search the carriage. After pocketing his items, however, the second man searched the carriage and found the crate under the blanket.

Edward stepped forward. "Please, that belongs to a ruthless man who will kill me if I do not bring it to him."

"That sounds like a personal problem." Both robbers laughed. The second man tied his horse to the back of the carriage and climbed into the driver's seat.

Edward made one last plea. "If they catch you with that item, Monsieur Bergeron will have you killed. You are better off without it."

The man whipped the horse and took off down the road, which opened up a short distance beyond the bend. The first man stood guard over them until the carriage was far enough away and then took off after his compatriot.

Edward and Davis walked back in the direction they had come under a brilliant sun that felt like a betrayal. The walking was slow. Their shoes and legs were covered in mud, and it took a full half-hour to reach the nearest farmhouse. The farmer pointed a shotgun at them and ordered them away. Edward told him of the robbery, and the farmer relented and gave them a ride into Metz. They went to the police station and reported the theft. Edward told the police sergeant about the crate and that it belonged to Monsieur Bergeron, who would pay a finder's fee to have it returned. They hired a carriage to take them back to Nancy, and Edward was almost more afraid of telling Catherine what had happened than he was for whatever hell Bergeron would rain down on him.

As they entered town, the long shadows of the buildings created a sharp contrast of warm sun and cold shade that reminded him of prison bars as they alternated down the street. It only stoked his fear of what Bergeron's wrath might bring.

When they had returned to their hotel, Edward gently knocked on Catherine's door while Davis returned to their rooms. When he went to his own room, Edward left the door ajar. He waited with trepidation, cringing in anticipation of her reaction.

She came in a few moments later. "Well?"

"We were robbed."

"What? Where?"

"Approximately one kilometer outside Metz. Two bandits came and stole not only our personal effects, but the carriage, and with it, the crate. We had a farmer deliver us to the police in Metz, where we reported the theft and told them Bergeron would offer a reward for the safe return of the crate."

Catherine stood, her jaw open, unable to absorb the ramifications of what he told her.

He continued, "There is nothing I can do about this, so I am going to continue our investigation. Whatever happens now is out of my control."

Catherine's eyes held a fear within them, which she resolutely refused to give voice to, but it expressed itself as a sadness, a hopelessness that he had never seen on her face before. She responded, "You are correct. There is nothing else to be done. If you will excuse me, I will return to my room to dress for dinner, assuming you would still prefer to dine together."

"Yes, I would prefer that. I will see you at eight o'clock."

They dined at a small restaurant tucked into the corner of a large building with a mansard roof and an arched entrance. The walls had frescoes of trees and beautifully colored birds flying across a blue firmament, and for a moment Edward forgot all that weighed on him and stared at the bird's tropical plumage. They sat at a table near the far wall with windows overlooking a park and trees shivering off the last of their leaves. During dinner, they discussed what they had learned. Catherine shared that she could not speak to Davet's mother, who was refusing visitors in her grief, nor Chloe, who was not home the two times she visited.

Catherine asked, "What should we do next?"

"I do not know quite what to do. If Henri was investigating Bergeron's stolen elephants, I suppose it might be a good idea to know more about his shipping operation here. Although, since I cannot safely visit his offices and speak to people, that likely has limited value. When I went to his warehouse, the man said, 'I was not expecting you until this evening. I wonder who he was expecting? Was it a black marketeer? A client? Bergeron's representative? It could have bearing on what happens next.'

"I have been thinking about the elephant," Edward continued. "It was pure jade. The cost must have been extraordinarily dear, and it was perhaps another artifact, like the larger elephants he showed me. I recall reading some literature on the discovery of a site in China by a group of Danish archaeologists. I do not recall the details, but the site had cultural significance, and I remember reading about jade statuary. Now perhaps I am grasping at straws, but perhaps the elephant came from China."

"And if it did? Are there laws against purchasing statuary from an archaeological site?"

"No. However, there are laws against theft, and many of these purchases start with a robbery."

"A robbery in China means nothing to us."

"True, but I would like to visit the warehouse tonight and watch their operation from outside the fence to see if something odd is going on there."

"Have you not had enough adventure for one day? Besides, what if someone recognizes you there? That warehouse is the last place you should be. Besides, you need rest."

"There will be no rest for me tonight no matter where I am. I would rather not be alone in the dark ensnared in my swirling relentless thoughts of...of...all that has brought us here." He paused, then continued, "I...I...cannot face that."

Catherine gently put her hand on his arm as he tried to avoid her gaze. "I am coming with you."

Chapter Sixteen

The melancholy that threatened Edward vanished, to be replaced by the fear of putting Catherine in danger. He met her gaze. "Absolutely not."

She threw her head back and set her arms akimbo. "Do not be foolish. My coming with you makes perfect sense. Have you ever seen a shipping yard? You will not know what you are looking at. Besides, if you think I am going to miss out on spying on my chief competitor's operation, you are quite mistaken. He recently built the port expansion with his warehouse here, since the old port was for sailing ships, not steamships. He worked with the city to finagle a deal where he helped pay for the public port renovation and received the land for a neighboring private port for his own operations in exchange. It is one of the few private ports in France. Shockingly, Napoleon III agreed to it, but Bergeron seems to have a special relationship with him."

"Your knowledge would be helpful, but I will not risk your safety."

"How many times must we have the same argument?"

"I am not arguing. I am simply—"

She cut across him. "Arguing. I have investigated with you many times, and this time my expertise will be invaluable. You know this."

Edward sighed. "All right."

Catherine's eyes were wide for a moment, startled. Edward too noted his swift acquiescence and mentally chalked it up to some lingering effects of his fever. They agreed to leave for Bergeron's after changing from their dinner clothes.

Once he was in dark clothes, Edward rented a small phaeton carriage from the hotel. He went to the stable to collect it and parked down the street.

He saw Catherine leave the hotel. She wore a dark serviceable wool dress that was as unremarkable as any woman's dress Edward had ever seen. She walked past him sitting in the carriage and on to the darker section of the street close to the gardens. There she waited for him to catch up to her.

When he pulled up, she got in, and soon they were outside of town and driving along the river. There was little traffic out here, and the night was clear, albeit chilly. The Milky Way seemed to lead them toward their destination.

Close to the warehouse, Edward found a dark field behind an old, weathered drying barn to tie off the horse and carriage. When they were within sight of the warehouse, they crept to the edge of the trees to remain hidden. The slowly rising moon provided a paucity of light that filtered through the pines as they entered the woods. The light from the shipping yard guided them through the trees, which stood like guards watching over the proceedings below. Edward was thankful their footsteps were quiet on the soft pine needles as they moved through the understory.

They likely could have been as loud as a herd of buffalo and still might have gone unnoticed, as the men in the yard below shouted instructions and the throaty belch of a steamship grew louder as it moved toward the only empty dock for unloading. There were eleven well-lit ships already unloading, with men moving cargo down long ramps and hoisting crates using block and tackle onto the wharf. Long horse-drawn carts moved crates around the wharf to what appeared to be designated storage areas. Great mounds of coal were on the far side of the main wharf, and at least two ships were being reloaded with coal for the next leg of their journey.

Edward and Catherine found a hidden spot amongst some myrtle bushes with a good view over the shipping yard and settled in. Catherine used her opera glasses to better view the works, while Edward looked through the field glasses he normally used for bird identification. He saw the longshoremen stack crates into different areas, presumably based on their next destinations, while the stevedores rowed cargo out to the waiting ships. Down to a man, they were all burly men with enormous arms and wide chests, many with beards. Edward watched as they singlehandedly carried crates as if they were toys. Given the hour, it surprised Edward how busy the site was.

"Are warehouses always this busy?"

"Oh yes. Even at four o'clock in the morning, it will be at least this busy. Shipping is one of the few businesses that operate around the clock."

Catherine continued to watch, shifting her weight as the time wore on. After two hours, Edward inquired if she had seen anything unusual. She had not, although she had seen some ideas she might put into practice to maximize efficiency in her own shipping operation. Cargo was unloaded and moved to storage locations, then after one ship finished, the next moved in. Edward counted at least three more ships waiting in the river. By eleven o'clock, Edward felt he had a good understanding of how a shipping yard operated, although he was sure Catherine would tell him otherwise.

Suddenly she gripped Edward's arm. "Hero is here."

"What?" Edward followed her gaze and pointed his field glasses to the back of the building. There was Hero shaking a man's hand before going inside. There was no mistaking him with his bald head, rotund figure, and solicitous smile. Edward even recognized his waistcoat.

"What in the world is he doing here? I thought he went to a vineyard?"

"I do not know; however, having my uncle cozying up with my chief competitor is not a sight I relish."

They watched for thirty minutes more before Edward saw Hero exit the front door. "He is leaving. He placed an envelope in his interior coat pocket."

Another man brought a horse to him and he rode away on the road to the north.

Edward, still watching Hero, asked, "Why is he traveling north?"

"He probably wants to avoid the appearance that he has been here, or perhaps he is returning to the vineyard he spoke of."

Catherine pursed her lips, clearly annoyed that her uncle was somehow involved with Bergeron's operation.

Edward rose. "Should we follow him?"

"Our time is better spent observing the warehouse. We will have plenty of time to watch Hero."

Edward sat down again and watched the yard for another hour, where operations were apparently normal.

Then Catherine gasped. "Look in the yard by the schooner near the end of the dock."

"Which is the schooner? I do not know the names of the various ship types."

Catherine pointed his field glasses toward the ship. "There. They are dragging that man off the ship. Do you see?"

Edward moved the field glasses back and forth until he saw the man being pulled along by two workers. They were laughing, joking with each other, one of his arms in each of their hands. His head slumped against his chest, and he had apparently passed out. His boots dragged on the ground, and one finally slipped off.

"We should do something." Catherine stood and started to walk away when Edward followed and grabbed her arm.

"No. Have you forgotten that Bergeron would be happy to put my head on a pike? We cannot be caught here."

"But that man is in trouble."

"And it is likely trouble he brought on himself."

"You mean as you did by stealing the elephant?" She wrested her arm from his grip.

"That was uncalled for." Edward's jaw hung open for a moment before he remembered to close it.

Catherine stopped and pointed her field glasses back to the shipping yard. "They are placing him in a crate! We must do something."

"No, we—"

Before he could finish, she was racing downhill.

Chapter Seventeen

"Get to the base of the hill," Catherine said to Edward as she ran toward the yard. "I will distract them. When you can, grab him and drag him away."

He ran forward through the trees and grabbed her. "Are you mad?"

She opened her mouth, and Edward's hand clamped tight upon it. "No. I cannot drag him back here." As Catherine's eyes grew wide, she thrust her tongue against his hand. He pulled it away and continued, "Not to mention that I am likely wanted for theft. Whatever that man did to get himself into trouble is none of our concern. If we get caught, it will be me in that crate."

Catherine pursed her lips and shot him a sideward glance as she straightened her skirt. "Fine. But other than Hero's presence, there is nothing suspicious."

Edward resumed watching the yard as she stood over him, pouting. The men roughly sealed the rough wooden crate with only a couple of nails, moved it to a staging area, and returned to work. "They have moved the crate to the base of the hill. If I am stealthy, I can release him."

"I will come with you."

"No, go back and hide in the woods near the carriage. If anyone approaches, flee in the carriage. I will be fine on my own."

Edward crept through the forest as quietly as he could. The fallen leaves, coupled with a recent rain, made the terrain slick, and he slipped several times on his journey to the base of the hill. He raced to the crate and pulled out the long knife he had brought, then began working the pins that held the crate together. As he worked, the wood squealed. He stopped and crouched down, peering through the slats of the crate as a longshoreman walked toward him. The man was lit from behind, his shadow looming larger and larger. Edward crouched lower so he could no longer see the man approaching through the crate because the body inside blocked his view.

He heard Catherine scream above him. The man stopped and ran toward the noise. Two other workers joined him, and they climbed the hill toward her scream.

Edward opened the crate and dragged the unconscious man into the woods. At the base of a large oak, he slapped the man's face until he awoke. He was unshaven, with a scruffy brown beard and unkempt hair. Edward wrinkled his nose at the stench of ale and vomit that wafted from him. His clothes looked as if he had slept in them for a week and were half covered in mud from the rough handling he received from his peers. Once he awakened, he was groggy, but he could move. Edward put the man's arm over his shoulder and half carried him away from the shipping yard into the woods.

He heard "No!" from Catherine and knew the men had caught her. The drunken sailor stopped, and Edward said, "You must help

me rescue her. She is the entire reason I pulled you from that crate."
The man nodded.

Edward devised a plan to surround the three men holding
Catherine and knock them out with rocks. He and the sailor slipped
through the woods and took their positions behind two trees to
launch their attack.

Edward could see them clearly from his vantage point. There were
three men surrounding Catherine. She stood tall, but Edward knew
she had to be terrified. Edward heard her explaining that she had
come alone to spy on her lover. None of the men believed her. She
looked too refined, too wealthy, too *clean*, to be a dockworker's
lover, but she was resolute in the story. One man toyed with her
hair as he said something that Edward could not quite hear. Edward
threw a rock at him, hard enough to make him stumble but not
knock him out.

Edward expected to see rocks coming from the man he rescued,
but none did. He crouched and saw the sailor he had saved was gone.
You should have known he would run. Edward snatched the closest
rocks and threw them at the other men, but only one rock found its
mark. The man pulled Catherine behind a tree while the other two
moved toward Edward, who crouched in a bush.

A cry went up from the yard as someone discovered the empty
crate. Several men began searching for the missing sailor. *Hopefully
he has not stolen my carriage,* Edward thought.

As the commotion continued, Edward stealthily crept up behind
the men holding Catherine. He grabbed the larger one and knocked
him out with one well-placed punch to the jaw. One of the other

men ran away, leaving only the third, who was holding Catherine. The worker laughed, and Edward watched helplessly as the man pulled her deeper into the woods.

The man called out, "Whoever you are, I've got your girl, but she won't be your girl when I'm done with her. I've got a knife to her throat, so you'll want to be staying back."

Edward crept to the man he had knocked out. "And I have your friend. We seem to be at an impasse."

The man chuckled. "Not my friend. More like my enemy. Kill him if you like. I have the better end of the deal."

Edward muttered to himself, "Clearly you do not know her."

He heard the man pulling Catherine through the woods and grunting. Catherine coughed a few times to let Edward know her location, and he followed until he found a spot below them in a copse of bushes where he could hide and wait for them. When he was close, Edward sliced his knife through the air, but the blow glanced past the man's shoulder. It was enough to loosen his grip on Catherine, and she grabbed a rock and struck her captor across the nose. The man howled with pain, and a shower of blood sprayed from his face. As he grabbed his face, Catherine ran uphill as fast as she could. Edward grabbed a large rock and knocked him out cold and then ran up the hill after Catherine.

They raced to the carriage, and Edward drove as fast as he could, pushing the horse faster with the whip. The thin pale moon provided the only light, which barely showed the road, let alone any rocks or other hazards. The carriage bounced and swayed as Edward swerved to stay within the curves of the road, and Catherine gripped the doorhandle with both hands to keep herself stable. In the darkness, he missed the first turn and drove into a field. The carriage shook violently, and Catherine's door swung open as the carriage tipped, almost spilling her out, but Edward grabbed her arm and leaned hard to the left to stop the carriage from flipping over entirely as he stopped the horse.

Edward made sure Catherine was all right then checked the horse's harness. Finally he listened in the darkness. He did not hear anyone following, and he relaxed as he lit the carriage lamps, guided the horse back onto the road, and resumed a safer speed. After a mile with no one following, he again slowed their pace, but Catherine still gripped the handle.

When they arrived at the hotel, Edward drove straight to the stables behind the building. It was very late, or very early, depending on your point of view. He handed Catherine out of the carriage and hugged her. He could feel her heart still racing against his chest and her soft breathing in his ear. Her arms wrapped tightly about his waist, and he smelled the faint scent of sweet olive blossoms in her hair. He inhaled the scent deeply, and they held each other before Edward broke the silence. "Thank God you are all right. You must have been so frightened. I should have never brought you."

Catherine pulled back. "Do not start with recriminations. We learned something important. I was frightened, but I believe I have shown I am not helpless."

"Indeed." Edward chuckled and pulled her close again. "Thank you for being so...capable."

CHAPTER EIGHTEEN

The next morning Edward startled awake to a slamming door somewhere nearby. He had been dreaming of Henri. They were in his cousin's house, a house they had visited together when they were at university. It was the house where Henri's great-great-grand aunt's body was kept. She had died decades before, and her will stipulated that she was to be placed upright in a glass-fronted coffin so her family could keep watch over her in case she awakened, not understanding that the embalming process would ensure she was dead. She was a wealthy eccentric, and her family played along thinking it was a joke—until they discovered that her will was ironclad. If the family wanted to inherit all her money, she would stay in this manner; otherwise, her fortune would go to the city to create a garden conservatory. The family received a stipend from her estate, and they made a small business of surreptitiously selling tickets for people to view her. Those in polite circles never spoke of it, of course, but everyone in Paris knew where to get a ticket to see her decomposing body.

In reality, their visit that summer had only been a short one. However, to Edward, it was one of the more bizarre experiences of his life. Henri had practically dared Edward to come with him to see her, calling it training as an archaeologist. As they approached her glass-fronted coffin surrounded by black crepe fabric, Henri tried to scare Edward with phantom touches to the shoulder. Edward walked up close to see her. Her dress was a bright vermilion with a voluminous skirt in the style of her time, as if she were going to the Danse Macabre, where skeletons escort the recently dead to their graves. Her nose was only an open socket, and her eyes were sunken into her head. Paper-thin skin stretched over prominent cheekbones. They had wired her hands together to hold a long-dead flower bouquet, where only the stems remained and the heads were dusty petals near her feet. It was the stuff of the worst of Grimm's fairy tales.

In his dream, Edward and Henri were in the coffin room. She was standing there waiting for their visit. As they approached, she spoke to Edward in an unintelligible tongue, raised her hand, and pointed at him. Her mouth twisted and her utterances became louder, more accusatory, more dire, the closer he got. Nothing she said made sense, but her words filled him with dread. It left him cold, and he huddled under his blankets, trying to put the dream out of his mind.

Soon thereafter, Davis came in and stoked the fire. When it was warmer, Davis dressed him, and Edward had an idea. "Davis, have you socialized with Hero's man?"

"A bit, but not much, sir."

"What type of individual is he?"

"His name is Reed. He is rather flamboyant for a valet and, well, I do not wish to speak out of turn...He is rather a gossip. Why do you want to know?"

"I went to watch Bergeron's shipping yard last night and saw Hero entering the building. I want to know more about him. Could you spend time with Reed to learn more about Hero?"

"Of course, sir. What would you like to know?"

"For right now, simply an understanding of Hero's comings and goings or any strange envelopes found in his clothing. I believe I saw him pocket one last night. Anything you might deem unusual about a man of his station. Consider this task of a higher priority than your normal duties. If you investigate, you do not need to attend to me."

"Of course, sir. I will inform you of my findings."

Edward met Catherine and Hero for breakfast in the inn's small dining room. Catherine looked remarkably well after the night's adventures, and even her dark mourning clothes looked fetching. Hero yawned and complained about not sleeping well, which was borne out by the bags beneath his eyes. His clothes were impeccable: a coffee-colored jacket and pants, and a gold pocket watch, which he checked frequently. Hero explained another local vineyard had invited him to diagnose their vines and excused himself.

Once alone with Catherine, Edward said, "I have asked Davis to get to know Hero's man to discover more about him. I know he is your uncle, but his apparent relationship with Bergeron is disconcerting."

"I wired my father first thing this morning to ask if he knew of any reason Hero would visit Bergeron's warehouse in the night. I will share any information he sends, but I assume he does not have a reason."

"Would you care to accompany me to Davet's house to pay our respects?"

"Of course."

A half-hour later, they were in a carriage driving to the Molyneux's home. The address was across town, and Catherine looked out the window as they rode. Edward studied the back of her head, noting the jeweled combs in her hair and the small cascade of curls covering the back of her neck. He imagined what kissing that neck might be like before chastising himself.

When they arrived, he assisted her out of the carriage. The home was a brown three-story building on a narrow street near the university. Black crepe surrounded a weathered royal-blue door, and the windows had their shutters closed and covered with black curtains that billowed softly in a way that seemed to dance in the breeze with their neighbor's colorful laundry hanging nearby. Catherine rang the bell, and a few moments later, a butler appeared.

"Hello, I am Catherine Briggs, and this is Sir Edward Tyrington. We are friends of Davet and came to express our condolences to Madame Molyneux."

The butler conducted them to a small waiting room next to the front door. The closed blinds kept the room dark, and there were candles and lanterns set on the two small tables in the room. Coupled with the dark mahogany walls and dark-colored sofa, the room appeared cave-like. Catherine sat in one of the two dark wooden chairs, and Edward paced the room. The room was spare, with few personal effects from the family except a framed honorarium for meritorious service from the university. The butler returned and led them to a study lined from floor to ceiling with books on three walls. Above the stone fireplace was a frame also covered in black crepe, which Edward assumed was a portrait of Davet.

Davet's mother, an elderly woman covered from head to toe in black, sat before the fireplace staring into the cold ashes of a long-dead fire. She barely turned her head when they entered the room. The butler cleared his throat and introduced them to Madame Molyneux.

Edward said, "We are sorry to intrude, but wanted to express our condolences over Monsieur Molyneux's death."

Davet's mother turned to them. Her eyes were red from crying, and the lines around her eyes and mouth were deep. Her mouth was a hard, thin line chiseled across her face, which had the look of cold marble. She was quiet for several minutes before she spoke. "Thank you." Then she turned her attention back to the cold fireplace.

Edward searched Catherine's face for a hint of how to proceed, but she seemed puzzled too. He cleared his throat. "Can you tell us about what happened?"

She appraised him and seemed to judge whether he was worthy of discussing such things with her. "It happened at the university. Davet was working late on his research. Apparently Monsieur Le Marchal was with him. The police believe it was Evaline who killed them. She disappeared the same night."

"Henri was with him at the lab?"

"Yes, Davet took him to see the project he was working on."
She broke down in tears, burying her face in a handkerchief. "I
apologize," she said, breathing deeply to compose herself. "If you
will excuse me, this has been very trying."

Edward bowed and again expressed their sympathies. As they
were leaving, Edward noticed the photograph of Evaline and Davet
on the piano. Her mouse-brown hair was tied in a loose bun on her
head, and she had a wide, toothy smile. She seemed very young.

The butler escorted them out, and they silently walked down
the street. Catherine broke their reverie.

"Would you mind walking back?"

Edward shook his head. "No."

As they walked, he asked, "Who would have wanted them
dead?"

"I do not know, but it was not Evaline. What if someone kidnapped her?"

"What if this is because of Henri?"

Catherine stopped and turned to Edward. "We should go to the
university. We need more information."

They changed direction and walked in silence down Leopold
Street. As they passed a small park, Catherine whispered, "Do not
look, but there is a man following us. He has followed us since we
left Davet's."

Edward leaned in. "Where do you see him?"

"To your right and slightly behind you. Do not look. Let us go
to the park and see what he does."

Edward followed her lead. She found a bench at the base of a statue of Napoleon. Before he sat, Edward looked up and remarked upon the large oak trees and their gold and orange leaves, then turned to see the man following them. As expected, he was behind them, but he walked past as they sat. The man had his collar pulled up against his face and his bowler hat pulled down low, but Edward could still see his prominent nose. He was not much older than Edward, and he was dressed in a drab gray coat, black pants, and scuffed boots.

Catherine whispered as she grabbed Edward's arm. "We should say something to him."

"What would you suggest?"

"Why are you following us?"

"And what if he lives here and his presence today is just happenstance?"

Catherine looked back and forth between the man and Edward. "And now he is getting away. What if he has information?"

"It seems unlikely that he would supply it after we accuse him of following us. Let us go to the university."

They resumed their walk and soon were at the university. The main building at the entrance to the campus was a four-story brick building with arched windows on the main floor and smaller windows on the floors above, and there were several other brick buildings situated around a central green area. Students walked in small groups huddled against the late afternoon breeze that was picking up. The medical arts building was the largest among them, with a clock tower protruding from the center of the building toward the sky.

Edward and Catherine entered through the double wood-and-glass doors and went upstairs to the department chairman's office. His door was open, and he sat at his desk with his head in his hands, his bald pate shining at them, surrounded by shelves of books, books haphazardly stacked on his small desk with papers folded and sticking out of the pages, and stacks of papers on the edge of the desk. There was also a half-drunk cup of tea and a plate of crumbs from a pastry.

Catherine knocked lightly on the doorframe. "Dr. Audibert, may we speak with you?"

He raised his head, his brown eyes vacuous, his chubby cheeks sagging like some kind of sad hound dog, the shadow of stubble showing on his chin. "Who are you?"

"I am Evaline Molyneux's cousin, Catherine, and this is a family friend, Sir Edward Tyrington."

"Do you know where she is?"

"No. I wish we did. Can you tell me what happened?"

"They were here at his laboratory. I found them at about two o'clock in the morning after hearing the shots."

Edward asked, "Any sign of who the culprit is? Did anyone see someone who did not belong on campus?"

"It was two o'clock in the morning. Everyone was asleep. There was no reason for them to be in the laboratory at such an hour. We have asked the students for information. No one has reported anything, including seeing strangers on campus that day or night.

The police questioned everyone, and other than them being, well, murdered—sorry, mademoiselle—and their notes being gone, there was nothing amiss."

Edward leaned forward. "Notes on what?"

"Davet had been working on experiments with medicine for heart arrhythmia." He chuckled sardonically. "I thought he would blow up the building rather than discover anything useful, but he had some promising results."

"Blow up the building? That seems unusual."

"The medicine contained a highly unstable substance that has a calming effect on the heart's rhythm. I know nothing more about it, though. Davet was always careful not to share details because he did not want his research stolen, and in this case, he was even more secretive. He refused to let his normal assistant work with him and insisted he do the work alone. He worked late at night to limit the possibility of hurting other people. It was that dangerous."

"Do you think someone was interested in his work?"

He nodded. "I know they were. Whoever did this ransacked Davet's office and many of his papers were stolen. We found his locked cabinet open and empty. Whoever did this found what they were looking for."

"Was he working with anyone else on this medicine?"

"He worked with a foreigner, but I do not know who. I also saw a woman in his lab once, but she was likely just a diversion."

Catherine's lips pressed into a fine line. "I see. Is there anything else?"

"Not that I can think of. We have shared everything with the police. You can ask them."

Edward asked if they could inspect Davet's laboratory, and Monsieur Audibert agreed.

CHAPTER NINETEEN

A student named Stefan walked with Edward and Catherine across the green and behind the economics building to a low brick building tucked at the edge of the woods.

"This seems an out of the way place for laboratory," Edward said, standing in the doorway. "Do you know why his lab was in this building?"

"No," Stefan replied. "This building used to be for storing records, but they moved Dr. Molyneux's lab in here about a year ago."

"Does anyone else work in this lab, aside from Dr. Molyneux?"

"No sir, this lab was only for his work."

Edward turned toward Catherine. "Perhaps..." He faltered. He did not want to push her into this just to prove something, but he knew this moment would be trying at best. "You may want to wait outside. This may be too much." Edward held his breath, waiting for her to straighten and tell him she was not some shrinking violet that needed to be handled gently.

Catherine looked at the ground. "You may be right. I will wait out here."

Edward felt the shock of her agreement color his face, but he tried to keep his expression neutral. He entered the lab with Stefan, who stood by the door and waited for him to complete his task.

The lab was in a long room with several long tables. One of the tables had cabinets beneath that extended along the outer wall and contained two plumbed sinks, a rather modern addition to what was clearly an older building. The floor was clean, and there were no footprints. There was a large chalkboard at the far end of the room that had two surfaces so you could raise one in front of the other. Edward started his investigation there. The boards had been wiped clean, but he closely inspected them to see if he could discern any words. In one area, he made out three C's in a triangle with dashes connecting them, but nothing more. It was part of a chemical formula, but this was probably one of the more common parts as it represented carbon, which most chemicals included. In the corner next to the chalkboard, he noted some brown flecks on the wall. He leaned in to inspect more closely. *Blood splatter.* He touched the wall. *Had Henri been standing here or Davet?* He pushed the thought from his mind and turned to face the rest of the room.

Edward walked along the bench; at the sink, he smelled something akin to burnt sugar. It reminded him of a cook his family had who had tried to make sweets for him and his brothers, but the fire was too hot. She had burnt the batch into a mess that was nearly impossible to remove from the pot. She did not last long as a cook for them, but he remembered her as one of his favorites because she once sent scones with clotted cream to his room. This smell here was not of a good caramelized sugar, though; it was the smell of sugar burnt to pure black. It was a faint smell, or it would be very unpleasant.

He asked the student, "Do you know what he might have been working on that would smell like burnt sugar?"

Stefan sniffed the air. "No. I am only a second-year student."

Edward crouched down to see if there was anything under the bench or sink that would produce that smell. He found nothing. As he scanned underneath the rest of the cabinets, he saw a piece of paper and the remains of what was likely a pool of blood. He inhaled sharply. He could see it in his mind: Davet at the chalkboard explaining his research, and Henri standing here watching. *Was he smiling, as he used to when he was learning something interesting?* He swallowed hard and pushed the image away. He jammed his fingers beneath the cabinet and barely got enough purchase to retrieve it. It was the beginning of a letter. The corner of the page was brown with dried blood.

Dear Alfred,

I am sorry, I must

There was nothing more. *Who might Alfred be?* Edward wondered. He asked if he could take the letter, and Stefan shrugged.

"Have you ever seen anyone here besides Dr. Molyneux?"

"I saw a girl come here sometimes. I do not know who she was, but perhaps she would know something."

"What did she look like?"

"She was older than me, but not by much. She was tall, like your companion, thin. I think she had blond or light hair, but she wore a bonnet, so it was hard to see. I did not see her face since I only ever saw her at night."

There was a glass cabinet in the corner that contained vials of chemicals. Edward noted the large bottles labeled nitric and sulfuric acid were nearly empty, while the others were mostly full. Edward opened the cabinet and saw a small corner of paper under the nitric acid bottle. He turned his back to the student to block his view and lifted the bottle. There was a small folded paper, and he slipped it into his pocket. He closed the cabinet and walked outside, the student locking the door of the lab behind them.

Edward asked, "Has the lab stayed locked since this happened?"

"Yes, sir. Monsieur Audibert has ensured we locked it and keeps the key himself."

Edward thanked him and looked around. Catherine was nowhere to be found.

"Did Miss Briggs tell you she was leaving?"

"No, sir."

He shielded his eyes against the sun and scanned across the green. But she was not there. He called her name, but she did not respond. *Where in the devil has she gone to now?* He walked around the laboratory building but did not see her. He walked to the economics building, which was closest to the lab, followed a student into the main hall, and called her name, but received no response. Edward asked the student if he had seen a woman on campus, but he had not. He crossed the green and asked other students that he passed if they had seen her, but none had.

At the entrance to the college, he glimpsed her walking north on the boulevard, away from the school. He ran down the street to catch her, finally calling out her name. She turned and entered a store about halfway down the block on the right. Edward raced there and threw the door open. She was standing just inside with a finger on her lips, shanks of meat hanging behind her. After having investigated the place where Henri died, it felt incredibly macabre, and a shiver coursed up his spine. Edward closed the door and joined her near the back of the butcher store.

"Where did you go? I was worried sick."

"I saw the man who was following us earlier. He was snooping near the edge of the woods by the lab, so I tried to follow him. I was doing well until you called my name and I had to hide in here."

"I am sorry to disrupt your investigation, but I did not know what happened to you and no one saw you leave."

"I apologize for that. The man following us was trying to look into the windows of the lab while you were in there. He was not some passerby who appeared to be following us; he clearly has an interest in our investigation."

They left the butcher shop and continued along in the direction the man had taken for a few more blocks to see if they could find him, but he was long gone. Eventually they took a carriage back to their inn.

As they rode, Edward asked, "Do you know of any friend or relation of Davet's named Alfred?"

"Not that I can think of. Why?"

"I found a note that said 'Dear Alfred, I am sorry, I must,' and that was all."

"May I see it?"

Edward thought of the blood-soaked corner. "Trust me, you would rather not. I also found this." He pulled the note from the chemical cabinet from his pocket and opened it. The handwriting was hastily scrawled in tiny letters.

C -

Do not follow me. We are in great danger. I am leaving tonight. Take care and tell no one.

D.

CHAPTER TWENTY

Edward handed the note he'd found in the lab to Catherine. "Davet knew he was in danger and planned to leave."

Catherine said, "And was likely notifying this Alfred of his intention to leave as well."

"Possibly. I found the note to Alfred under a cabinet, so it may have been older, but that note also looks hastily written, so you may be right. Who is C? He left that for someone who would be in his lab, which shows C might be someone from the university."

"And why were they in great danger? Was it because of their research or something else?"

"C might know the answer to that."

"I really do not know any of Davet's friends to comment on who might have a name that begins with C. Perhaps there is a Charles or a Clement."

Edward turned toward Catherine. "Everyone at the university that we spoke to has said they knew nothing of his research, indicating that they were not regularly in his lab. However, twice now, people have mentioned a woman in his lab. The student who accompanied me said she was tall, and he thought she had blond hair. Could there be a mistress?"

"Out of the question. He adored Evaline." She turned away from him to look out the window.

"He was also French. Are mistresses not de rigueur?"

Catherine faced him and pursed her lips. "That is such a cliché. Not all French men cheat on their wives."

"You have a wide circle of married acquaintances. How many do you know that do not have a mistress at least rumored to be in their lives?" Edward smirked.

Catherine sat silent for a full minute, chewing her lip. The gears of her mind were clearly grinding in an attempt to name at least one. She finally gave up. "I am sure there are many."

Edward's smile broadened. "Just as I thought. Following that information, is there a woman you know with a name that begins with C?"

"Chloe Bellon. She was at the funeral. She is also blond. But she is Evaline's second cousin; she would not dare."

"She is also tall, as I recall."

Catherine nodded and knocked on the front of the carriage to get the driver's attention. "We need to change our destination to rue Sellier."

"To Davet's house?"

"Yes. Hopefully someone there will know where Chloe lives, or who another C-named friend might be."

Davet's house was a quaint, nondescript cottage of brick with the doorways and windows draped in black. The front garden was spectacular, however, even in the late fall. Two sugar maples blazed deep red with late-blooming yellow mums shrinking from the cold. As they pulled up, his cousin Matilde was walking out.

Catherine scurried out of the carriage before Edward could open the door for her and said, "Excuse me, Matilde, may we have a moment of your time?"

Edward paid their driver as Matilde walked over. She did not appear as old as she had at the funeral when she wore what seemed to be mountains of black veils and crepe. She still wore black, but today she was in a simple walking dress. Her face was round with a wide-eyed expression that exhibited a general wonder about the world, giving her a more innocent appearance. Her hair was mousy brown and pulled back into a severe bun that clashed with her moonlike face, and she strode with purpose as opposed to the languorous walk most ladies exhibited. She walked like a woman who had somewhere to be and was likely already late.

"You may not remember me. My name is Catherine Briggs. I was a friend of Davet and Henri. We met last summer."

"I recall. I appreciate you traveled all this way for the funeral." She turned and gazed at Edward.

He doffed his hat and said, "Excuse me, my name is Sir Edward Tyrington."

Catherine continued, "We were glad to attend. It was all so sudden and completely unexpected. Henri's family asked if we might inquire what happened, and we recently found a link between Davet and someone whose name begins with C. I was wondering if you might know anyone who fits that description?"

Matilde looked puzzled. "I am not sure what you mean by 'inquiring what happened.' That seems beneath a woman of your station. Besides, I presume the police are investigating, although we have heard nothing from them. As for friends with a name beginning with C, the only one that comes to mind is Caine Reinard. He is a friend of Davet's father and was too frail to attend the funeral."

Catherine nodded. "Thank you. I am sorry to hear he could not attend the funeral." She leaned in closer and continued in a quieter voice, "I was also wondering what you know about Chloe."

Matilde stepped back and hissed, "Do not say that lying wench's name in my presence." She turned to Edward. "Please excuse my language, but there is no other word for her."

Edward smiled. "No apology necessary, but I am curious what she has done to cause such a statement."

Matilde's shoulders squared, and she filled her lungs as if preparing to deliver a long dissertation on the crimes of Chloe, but she only said, "She has spread lies about my brother. She has for years, and she continues to this day. But I have made sure the women of my circle know just how low she is. She is the worst kind of woman, not a lady at all."

Catherine's expression took on a sympathetic look. "Do you know where she lives?"

"She lives on rue Villard, near the railroad tracks, number 201. Not a place a lady would be seen, if you take my meaning."

Edward turned his head to look down the street. He smirked as he thought of Catherine skulking through the night dressed in a flowing white galabia in the Egyptian worker encampment earlier this year. He was certain the presence of the railroad nearby would not dissuade her from visiting Chloe's less than desirable home.

Catherine thanked her, and Matilde entered her carriage and left.

They inquired with Davet's butler and his mother if they recalled any friends with a name beginning with C, and Caine was the only one they too recalled. Edward and Catherine both agreed that between Chloe and Caine, Chloe seemed the more likely recipient for the note.

Edward pulled a dour face. "I am sure you will not want to investigate near the railroad tracks."

Catherine laughed. "If I recall correctly, that is also near the south cemetery. Most ladies only dream of having so much fun."

CHAPTER TWENTY ONE

They arrived at Chloe's house after dark. The street was narrow, and the buildings were tightly packed against one another. Even outside, it felt claustrophobic and unwelcoming, although both Edward and Catherine had been in much worse areas. Edward could see the railroad tracks at the far end of the street. A few people milled about, and the shops along the street were closing. They found her building, a short brick affair with small windows. Edward saw one light in the eastern window of the second floor, and he could make out the outline of a person behind the draperies. He and Catherine climbed the freshly painted stairwell. It was crisp white and, with its bright gaslights, it had a cheery aspect that gave Edward hope that Chloe's living conditions were not as dismal as Matilde had implied.

Edward knocked on the door, but no one answered. He whispered to Catherine, "I saw someone's shadow in the front room of this apartment from the street."

Catherine nodded and knocked again, saying, "Chloe, it is Catherine Briggs, Evaline's friend."

The door flew open, and she said, "Oh thank God!"

Chloe was tall, almost as tall as Catherine, and she had blond hair tied in a braid that snaked down the right side of her body almost to her midriff. She wore a black dress that hung off her like a sack. Mourning etiquette required ladies to purchase new outfits for each mourning period, however, it appeared that Chloe had ignored that tradition and she had lost weight since she last wore the dress. Quite a bit of weight.

She spotted Edward and said in French, "Who is this?"

"My apologies, this is Mr. Tyrington. He was a friend of Henri le Marchal."

Chloe spoke in a flurry of French. "Are you mad? You brought an English lord here? How well do you know him?"

"He is not a lord, and I know him very well. Also, he speaks French and can understand you." Switching to English, she continued, "Now please let us in. We have much to discuss."

They entered the small apartment. The faded draperies were closed. The dingy wallpaper was yellowed, and its green vine pattern was faint. There were ornate, Queen Anne-style wooden chairs by the fireplace, which held a blazing fire, and a rough wooden floor with no rug. A small polished-cherry tea cart was between the fireplace and the tiny galley kitchen. There were shelves near the fireplace, and a small porcelain doll in an ornate ball gown stood in the center of one shelf. A closed door to what was presumably a bedroom was off to the left. Edward noted the expense of some furnishings juxtaposed with the general shabbiness of the apartment.

Chloe poked her head out the door to scan the stairwell before closing it. She stood with her back to the door for a moment and then seemed to collect herself with a sigh. Her face seemed gaunt, whether from crying or lack of sleep Edward was unsure.

"I apologize. I have forgotten my manners. Please sit." She forced a smile. She pulled a newspaper off one of the wooden chairs by the fireplace and scuttled it on the bottom shelf of the nearby tea cart. "Can I offer you tea?"

Catherine sat. "No, thank you. We came to discuss recent events with you."

After Chloe pulled up a third chair from her small kitchen table, Edward joined them and said, "Miss Briggs and I are looking into what happened."

Catherine shot him a sideways glance as if to say, *Let me do the talking.*

Catherine leaned toward Chloe. "It is terrible what happened, and we are just trying to make sense of it all." She looked down and smoothed her skirt. "Davet was such a wonderful man, and I felt as if both he and Henri were brothers to me. I cannot fathom either of them having enemies, and now some are saying Evaline had something to do with it, which seems preposterous!"

Chloe relaxed a bit into her chair. "It *is* preposterous. She had nothing to do with this."

"Do you have any idea who might have?"

Chloe stood again. "No." She paced around the room and slowed as she passed the door. She cocked her head toward it as if she were listening for sounds in the stairwell.

Edward stole a glance at Catherine, who had a puzzled expression and a knitted brow.

Chloe rejoined them. "No, I am sorry. I wish I did."

Catherine put her hand over Chloe's. "Forgive me for saying so, but you seem nervous. Is there something wrong?"

Chloe stood, walked to the door again, listened, then came back. "Can I trust you? I have no one to trust, and I need help."

"Of course."

"I do not know who killed Monsieur Molyneux, but I know more about what he was up to than most people, even his wife."

Edward interjected. "Was it you visiting him at his lab?"

"How did you know about that?"

Catherine went to the spirits table and poured three glasses of sherry. Handing one to Chloe, she said, "A student saw you one night. Based on his description, we thought it might have been you."

Chloe sipped the sherry and nodded. "It was. I needed money, and he was paying me to help him in the lab."

Edward handed her the note he had found under the bottle. "Then I believe this note is for you."

She read it, and her mouth fell open. "I knew it. I knew they did this over his work. Mind you, I'm no chemist, so I do not know most of what he was doing, but I know it was dangerous."

Edward asked, "If you do not mind me asking, if you are not a chemist, why did he hire you?"

"He didn't need technical help. He needed someone to help take notes and clean things up. Sometimes Evaline would help him, but he didn't want to put her in danger, so he asked me. He told me once that he liked to have women assist him because if a woman stole his work, no one would believe them if they tried to sell his discoveries as their own."

"You did not mind the danger?"

Chloe looked at the floor and spoke in a softer, more shameful tone. "I needed the money. I was wealthy once, but my family suffered a series of setbacks. He paid me well."

"Do you know what he was working on, or with?"

"No. Not really. He was working on a heart medicine."

Catherine leaned forward. "Did you keep a copy of his notes?"

"No. They are in a locked cabinet in the laboratory."

"I am sorry to say that all the notes from the lab are gone. Can you recall anything of importance about his discoveries?"

Chloe drank her remaining sherry in one gulp and paced the room again, pausing near the door to listen before she answered. "He had been working on a new formula. About two weeks ago, he seemed to hit just the right combination. He sent Alfred a wire about it."

"Do you know who Alfred is?"

"I don't know his last name, but he lives in Prussia—Bonn, to be exact. I thought it odd that he was working with a foreigner."

Edward stood and peeked around the edge of the curtain. A man stood in the shadows of the building across the street. He could barely make him out, but he saw the top of his hat. The man looked up and Edward stepped back. "Chloe, I do not wish to alarm you, but we should leave here. If there is anything you must have, please get it quickly and let us go. Now."

Catherine looked at him, puzzled, and Edward twitched his head toward the window. Catherine stood and guided Chloe by the arm.

Chloe said, "Let me pack a few things. It will only take a moment." She closed herself in her room.

Edward whispered to Catherine about the man watching the building. "We will need to leave by the back door."

Chloe returned with a small, frayed, maroon carpet bag, and they exited through the back garden to an alley. As they reached the end of the alley, Edward looked back and saw a man dart from the shadows.

"I believe we are being followed. Is there a shortcut to the main road?"

Chloe nodded as they rounded the corner onto another alley, and she quickly led them to another turn.

Edward said, "I will stay here and see if I can divert him. Catherine, take Chloe to the hotel."

Catherine and Chloe ran down the alley and turned down another as Edward waited in the shadows for the man to catch up. Their pursuer rounded the corner and, seeing no one, stopped. It surprised Edward that he did not run after the women, but rather the opposite. He stood for a moment, looking down the alley, then turned back the way he came.

Edward waited a moment then slipped from the shadows and quietly made his way to the corner. He crouched behind a set of stairs, doffed his hat, and peeked around the corner and down the street. The man was nowhere to be seen. *He is waiting for me to show myself. This is not his first time following someone.* Edward remained crouched and listened for footsteps. After five minutes, when he still heard nothing, he peeked again. He saw no one. Edward waited another ten minutes, listening, and still saw no one.

He turned down the alley to follow Catherine and Chloe. He was happy to find that the alley gave onto a major thoroughfare, and he hired a carriage.

Arriving at the hotel, he confirmed that Catherine and Chloe were there. Catherine was helping Chloe get settled in her room, and Edward decided Chloe might be more forthcoming without his interference. He returned to his own room for the night.

CHAPTER TWENTY TWO

Davis had left a note that he had gone out with Reed. Edward settled in before the fire with an overly full glass of whiskey, watching the flames dance like an Egyptian girl. He mulled over what he had seen at the university, the puzzle of who Alfred was, and where Evaline had gone. After he poured himself another whiskey, his mind failed to keep his train of thought. He held his whiskey glass between his face and the flames to watch the fire through the liquid. Anything to keep his mind occupied.

Nighttime had been hardest since the news of Henri—the time spent alone in the quiet with nothing but his thoughts to fill the minutes, each marching slowly after the other in relentless succession. Tonight began as the others had, with an ache over the loss of Henri, but shifted to a deep simmering anger at himself. Why had he not been with Henri? Why had he not been there to protect him as Henri had protected Edward? And finally, *What hope do I have of solving Henri's murder and bringing the perpetrator to justice?* Henri had always been better at puzzling than Edward. Henri was the one Edward's father had always been proud of. Edward chastised himself for focusing on the jealousy that he knew had always been there, a riptide underneath all the love. He loved Henri like the brother he wished he had. Now he only had Charles as his sole remaining family. Certainly things could be worse, but between the lack of funds, the current lack of job, the lack of family, and, of course, the lack of skills to avenge his best friend's murder, he was not sure exactly how they could be worse. He poured himself another whiskey and hoped to forget.

Edward awoke at three o'clock in the morning, still sitting in the chair. The fire grate before him was cold. The draperies were open, and the moon was waxing pale and setting over the river. At first Edward was unsure why he had awakened, but soon he heard a series of thumps in Davis's room. He rose. The room was chilly, and he rubbed his arms and gently knocked on Davis's door.

"Sir, I am not fit to serve you at the moment," he slurred.

Edward opened the door a small crack. "I do not wish to disturb your revelry, but I was curious how it went."

Davis fell as much as sat on the bed. "I do not wish you to see me. I am quite drunk, sir."

"I will not judge you by anything you say or do tonight. Did you learn anything about Hero?"

Davis struggled to remove the buckhorn buttons from his shirt. "I learned nothing except that he is adept at navigating the low places in a town, and that he has certain 'proclivities.'"

"I am afraid to ask."

"It is best if you don't." Davis cradled his face in his hands. "And I would rather not have to explain it."

"As long as it does not bear on what business he had at Bergeron's warehouse."

"None, sir. Now may I sleep?"

"Of course." Edward went to the door and asked, "Is Hero back in his room, or is he still out?"

"I left Reed and Hero at a place I would rather not name. Reed knew Hero was there, and wanted to *spy* on Hero." The word "spy" tumbled from his mouth in a cavalcade of consonants and drama.

"Thank you. Sleep well. I will dress myself in the morning." Edward returned to his room and fumbled through his travel case for his lockpicks.

He swiftly picked the lock on the door to Hero's room and let himself inside. The room was messy, with shoes lying about, dirty glasses on the table along with two empty wine bottles, and everything in disarray. *Apparently Reed does very little for Hero. I wonder why he keeps him on?* He lit a small candle and looked for his traveling desk. It, too, was locked, and no amount of work with the picks would open it. Edward poked through the clothes that were lying about, as well as Hero's wine suitcase. He found nothing unusual.

Edward took the candle and moved into Reed's small adjoining room. The room was full of Hero's trunks and wardrobes with a small cot in the corner. He opened the wardrobes and looked for an overcoat. He finally found one amongst the unwashed laundry. There was mud on the hem. *Likely from his trip to the warehouse.*

He plunged his hand into the left pocket, which was empty. He tried the right pocket and came up with a small paper with Bergeron's watermark: a large red ornate B. The page said, "Pay 300 bar" with "150 paid" written across it. Edward returned the receipt to the pocket and dropped the coat onto the pile of laundry. He went to the wardrobe filled with jackets and searched those pockets. He found a small token with the word *Premiere* stamped into it. Edward took the token and closed the armoire. He snuffed the candle and left. It was not long after he heard stumbling in the hall and surmised that one or both of them had returned.

CHAPTER TWENTY THREE

The next morning Edward awoke early despite his drinking and late-night investigation. He studied a map of the town until breakfast time then went down to the dining room.

The room was airy, with large windows on the outer wall overlooking the river. Boats glided by, some carrying goods, while others were fishing or pleasure crafts. Catherine sat at a table near the window, the morning light shining off the red in her hair and shaming the sun with its radiance. The navy of the tablecloth made the blue of her eyes appear more like the ocean, briefly reminding Edward of their time sightseeing on Santorini.

Edward joined her. She informed him that Chloe was still sleeping but had promised to stay in Catherine's room in case whoever had been following them found her. He caught her up on Davis's exploits and explained that Hero would likely not awaken until the afternoon.

After their food arrived, Edward placed his new clue on the table in front of Catherine. "Do you know what this is?"

She picked it up and inspected it. "Some kind of token. Where is it from?"

"I found it in Hero's jacket pocket last night when I searched his room."

Catherine's eyes grew wide. "You did what?" Her voice took on a strident tone as she said, "Are you mad? What if he had caught you?"

"I had it on good authority that he would not return for some time."

"That is unacceptable. He is still my uncle."

"Who is, according to evidence I found, being paid by Bergeron. Someone has to find out what he is up to. It might as well be me. He did not return until after four in the morning. Long after I had left."

"I dislike you investigating him, but you are right, he is up to something and we need to figure out what."

Catherine presented the day's paper to Edward and pointed to a personal advertisement. "I placed a personal ad yesterday; it is in today's paper."

Edward read aloud: "'V.V. Ya meet me where D asked at eleven o'clock in the morning.—CB.' What is this?"

Catherine took the paper and pointed again. "Viviya is the nickname we had for Evaline as children."

"And you think she will both read the personal ads and interpret V. V. Ya as Viviya?"

"Of course, especially since I mention 'where D asked.' If she is here in town, she will go to Nancy Cathedral square at eleven a.m. She religiously reads the personal ads. She loves to imagine the stories behind some of them. It is her own creative entertainment. If she is still in Nancy, she will see this advert, and she will certainly know who CB is."

"And if she does not come?"

"Then we will go to Davet's house and ask her family for every scrap of information they have on where she has gone or what happened to her."

"What about Evaline's family? Does she have some relations here in town?"

"No. Her family is southeast of here in Lunéville."

Edward folded the paper and nearly choked on his almond croissant. The major headline on the front page said, "Bergeron Pays Reward to Police for Returning Stolen Elephant." It went on to describe the capture of two men near Metz who apparently had quite a stash of stolen goods, including a golden elephant that belonged to Gaston Bergeron. He paid the police 100 francs for the capture of the criminal and return of the golden elephant.

"A hundred francs seems rather stingy for what they returned to him," Edward said.

"He did not become as rich as he is by giving money away."

"True. Still," Edward smiled, "this means I am no longer on the hook. They found the robbers. He got his goods back. All is well."

Catherine shot him a sideward glance. "He did not become this rich by being magnanimous either."

Edward frowned at his plate. They finished their breakfast in silence, then agreed to meet at ten o'clock to get to the square early.

CHAPTER TWENTY FOUR

Davis awoke looking much worse for wear, with buttons misaligned and his shoes scuffed from the night before. He apologized for not serving Edward that morning even as Edward poured him a cup of tea with two lumps of sugar and set it before him. Edward apologized for asking Davis to find out more about Reed. Clearly Reed and Hero's lifestyle was more than either Edward or Davis could stomach. Edward told him he could cease the activity. Davis appeared to be grateful and sipped his tea.

Edward asked, "Do you know of any potential heart medicine that is made from a dangerous substance to work with?"

"Now may not be the best time to ask me such a question, sir."

"I am sorry." Edward went to his bedroom to prepare to meet Catherine.

As they drove to Nancy Cathedral square, Edward said to Catherine, "There is something that has been bothering me since the beginning of this. What was Henri doing working for Bergeron?"

"We already know that: looking for elephants."

"Yes, but why? Why was he working for him to begin with? His family has money and position. He was working in Egypt. Why did he leave that job? He gave a reason that seemed odd when I asked him, something about abhorring the desert, and then he changed the subject. Why was he doing things for Bergeron when, in reality, he did not need to work at all? It is not as if the le Marchals are poor."

"I do not know, but I do know Bergeron was the most vocal opponent to allowing those who had opposed Napoleon III to return, especially regarding the le Marchal family. I recall Henri telling me snippets of conversations he had eavesdropped on where Alfonse related some of what Bergeron had to say about his family. He was uncomplimentary in the extreme and deadly opposed to Alfonse being allowed back into France. Then, seemingly overnight, he supported ending exile for them and others. I do not know what happened, but it is likely there is history there, possibly a debt owed. Clearly, Henri had investigative skills, just as you do."

My father's lasting legacy, teaching spy craft to Henri and me.

"That is it!" Edward's voice dropped to a whisper. "I would bet that Henri was working as a spy. Possibly for the French government. That is why his family was allowed back. They provided information to Napoleon. Perhaps he was ordered to find Bergeron's goods."

"And perhaps he was sent to find out more about Davet's associations with a certain foreigner."

"Almost certainly. I believe that association had more far-reaching ramifications than he realized."

Edward leaned back and mulled over the idea of Henri being a French spy. It would make sense that they sent him to work for the Suez Canal Company in Egypt. The government had spent massive amounts of money and political capital pushing the project for de Lesseps. It would make sense that they would send him to make sure their money was being spent wisely, especially after the project had fallen so far behind. Then his heart sank. *I wonder if he used his connection to my father to give France English political secrets?* He pushed the thought away. He tried to recall their conversations and could not come up with anything that appeared to be political secrets. He determined that his father was almost certainly careful and had divulged nothing.

They disembarked across the square from the cathedral to watch the area for a while. The square was mostly empty for such a bright day, leaving the market sellers to converse with each other. The cathedral was in the late Baroque style, with two sets of stacked columns on either side of the main entrance for the three main stories, culminating in a large clock tower with a cross on top. Two bell towers rose above that on either side, with spires that reached still higher. There were balconies across the front of each level that Edward imagined had a commanding view of the town.

They strolled leisurely around the edge of the square, watching and waiting for eleven o'clock. There was a bakery near the market area and several other shops, including a cobbler, a haberdashery, and a barber across the way. The square had five entrances, one on either side of the cathedral, two from streets in the middle of the square, and one opposite the cathedral. Edward scanned each to see if a lone woman stood nearby, but found none. He and Catherine found a park bench and waited until the appointed time, then they walked to the cathedral. There was no one out front, and after waiting a few minutes, they circled the building. Evaline was not waiting when they returned to the front door, so they ventured in.

Inside the door stood a fountain of holy water. Catherine dabbed her finger and made the sign of the cross. Edward resisted the training of his youth and bypassed the fountain altogether. There was a series of arches on either side with clerestory windows that poured sunlight onto the few people sitting in the pews. The organ pipes, which hovered over the altar, dominated the sanctuary. The lower set of pipes were in five clusters centered over the altar table, and above those was another cluster of seven sets of pipe, which spanned from wall to wall. Edward tried to imagine the soul-shaking sound the pipes would produce and stood in awe for a moment, until Catherine prodded his elbow and indicated they should investigate. Edward told her to look around and that he wanted to watch the room from a dark corner. She walked up the eastern side of the church, while Edward kept close to the outer wall of the aisle, which was beyond the nave and unlit by the clerestory above. He found a column near the central transept and waited beside it, watching the door and the room.

There were only a half dozen worshippers since it was a weekday, and they all seemed quite old. Edward realized it rankled him to be in a church again. He disliked them as a matter of course, but the recent memory of Davet's funeral left him even less enamored to stand inside another one. He watched Catherine make her way around the nave, looking at each person as surreptitiously as possible. She was doing a good job of it—no long stares, and she made it look as though she were taking in the architecture as she scanned them. She really was much more adept at investigating than he gave her credit for. Watching her from a distance, without carrying on a conversation with her, his heart opened. He recalled staring into her eyes, watching her. *Had it only been two days ago?* He forgot their mission entirely and just stared at her as she moved from the light of the clerestory, which cast her hair in fiery hues of golden red, to the shadows, where she was only an outline in her dark mourning clothes. He stayed in his reverie until she rejoined him.

"She is not here."

Edward crooked his arm, and she let him escort her back out into the square. The sunlight was bright, and Edward looked toward the west side of the cathedral to shield his eyes. It was there he saw him. The man who had been following them the previous day.

Chapter Twenty Five

E dward leaned toward Catherine. "We are being followed again. I would like to see if I can follow him, but I do not wish to put you in jeopardy."

"If I walk in areas that have people, I should be fine. Perhaps if we make it seem as if we are parting ways, he will follow one of us."

"I do not care for it, but I also do not see how we will find out who he is without more information."

Before there could be more deliberations, she turned to him and fairly shouted, "All right then, I will meet you later," and turned and walked away.

Edward said, "Stay near the square," in a low voice. He had no choice but to turn the opposite way and try to get a bearing on where their pursuer was. Edward caught a brief glimpse of him in the haberdashery's doorway and picked up his pace toward the closest exit from the square. He rounded the corner and went into the nearest store with a glass front. It was a wire office, and he pretended to write a note while watching the window. After two minutes with no sign of the man, he peeked out of the door. Still not seeing him, Edward assumed he had followed Catherine and returned to the square.

He saw neither of them there, so he walked to the nearest boulevard off the square. He found Catherine sauntering down the street window shopping, but there was no sign of the man who'd been following them. He waited several minutes as Catherine made her way to the end of the second cross street—still no sign of the man. *Damn. We lost him.*

Edward caught up to Catherine. "He is more savvy than I thought and followed neither of us."

"If we have lost him, let us go to Davet's house and see what we can find out about Evaline."

Davet's butler lead them into a small library, where his mother sat clad in black before a cold hearth. Her eyes did not leave the ashes as they entered, and she did not notice them or acknowledge their presence. Edward cleared this throat, but still there was no response. He looked at Catherine and shrugged. Catherine approached her and knelt between her and the fireplace.

"We are sorry to disturb you, Madame Molyneux, but we have some questions regarding Evaline."

A sigh escaped Madame Molyneux's mouth, but nothing more.

Catherine continued, "We were wondering if she left of her own volition."

Madame Molyneux rotated her head to face Catherine as if she had just seen her for the first time. "Exactly what do you mean?"

"Did she take clothing? Or, perhaps, did her room appear to be searched?"

"She took her clothing. A small bag's worth." She called for her butler, who entered the room silently. "Take them to Miss Young. They have questions for her."

Catherine stood and thanked her before they followed the butler out. He asked them to wait in a small anteroom off the hall and several minutes later brought a small, mousy young woman to them.

Edward let Catherine take the lead since she was less intimidating than he.

"Good afternoon, we are sorry to disturb you. We had asked some questions of Madame Molyneux, and she directed us to you. May I ask, what is your role in the house?"

"Madame Molyneux's lady's maid. Excuse me. The younger Madame Molyneux." She gave a small curtsy.

"Do you know if she packed a bag when she left? Or did her room appear to have been searched?"

"Are you with the police?"

Edward interjected, "No. But someone asked us to assist in the investigation."

"Oh, a woman investigator, that's a lark." Then she covered her mouth. "Excuse me, miss."

Catherine smiled. "Innit though?" and gave the woman a wink.

The maid's eyes turned as big as saucers, and Catherine responded to the look. "I spent a fair bit o' time in the kitchen, if you catch my meaning. But what I need to know is this: did the madame pack a bag or did it look like, perhaps, she got kidnapped?"

"Oh thank you, miss! I've been saying the whole time it ain't right, but nobody will listen. Her room was a bit of a jumble. Not so bad, really, unless you knew her. She never left a thing out of place. Ever. When I come in the morning, there was a petticoat on the ground, and her combs were on the floor too. The police said she was rushing to pack her bag after she done the deed, but there's no way she done it. And there's no way she left her room like that. Something happened to her. And here's the other odd thing, if you don't mind me saying: she packed oddly." She shot a glance at Edward and motioned for Catherine to lean in, then whispered, "She took two walking dresses and a ball gown, but she only took one petticoat, no corset, and no crinoline. How was she supposed to wear her clothes with half of 'em missing? She also only took one hat."

Catherine leaned back from her. "I see. She take anythin' else?"

"Her writing desk. That was it."

"If she had run away, have you got any idea where she might have gone?"

"None, miss, but I can assure you, she did not run away. She loved Monsieur Molyneux. True love, you know? And she would not leave in this dark hour, especially when it was time to lay him to his eternal rest. No. Something bad has happened. I know it."

Catherine slipped a silver franc into her hand. "Thank you for taking the time to talk to us."

When they returned to the hotel, Edward returned to his room, while Catherine went to collect Chloe. They agreed to meet in the dining room in a half hour.

Davis looked like himself, although Edward noted he moved slower this afternoon.

"I apologize, Davis. Had I known the type of person Reed was, I never would have suggested you spending time with him. You do not need to do that again."

"Thank you, sir. He invited me to come out again tonight. Apparently, I am the life of the party, but I told him I needed to attend to you."

"I have a request. If you could find out the fastest way to get to Bonn and what time, I would appreciate it. I believe we have done all we could here."

"All right, sir. Also, you had asked me about heart medicine. Something dangerous, or even explosive. It occurs to me I have heard of some success using nitroglycerin to regulate a heart with an irregular beat."

"Well, that would certainly explain Davet's safety concerns. How well researched is this?"

"Barely at all. You can imagine how few would want to experiment with it. It is extremely unstable to handle."

Edward met Catherine and Chloe in a dark corner of the dining room. Catherine shared with Chloe the events of the day and a summary of everything Evaline's lady's maid had told them.

When she finished, Edward said, "Although I cannot confirm it, I could swear that the man who has been following us is the same man I saw outside your apartment, Chloe. Now perhaps he followed us there, or perhaps he is also following you, but we cannot continue to take chances. I do not know if the man following us is an employee of Bergeron or related to our investigation, but it is clearly not safe here for us. And if he were an employee of Bergeron, I doubt he would still follow us after they returned the elephant, which leads me to think he is investigating—or involved with—Davet's murder. I suggest we go to Bonn to find Alfred."

Chloe piped up. "I agree. I think that is our best option for finding Evaline and possibly who did this."

Catherine said, "I am not entirely convinced that Bergeron does not employ him, but it may be as you say. I think it is safe to say Evaline is not here in Nancy, but are you sure there is no one else we should speak to?"

Edward asked, "Who? I can think of no one."

Catherine chewed her lip. "I do not know. I just want to make sure." After a few moments she continued, "All right, we should depart."

Chapter Twenty Six

The next morning, they boarded a paddlewheel riverboat with two levels of rooms, a wide teak deck, two smokestacks, and a plethora of flags, both French and Prussian, at the fore and aft. The ship's name was *Benediction*, and despite his lack of faith, he accepted it as a good omen that they were on the right track. As Davis unpacked the few outfits Edward would need for the two-day journey, Edward went to the main lounge near the bow of the ship. The morning was bright and clear, and as the sailors pushed off from the dock, Edward stood by the rail, enjoying the breeze in his hair. Two members of the crew coiled lines nearby, and he overheard their conversation.

"The *Jean Per* made Bonn in thirty-eight hours. Captain wants to beat her record. I expect we'll be working without food or sleep tonight."

Edward asked, "Is this ship in a race?"

The sailor did not look up from his work. "Of a sort. The steamships are always trying to beat each other's time. Many of the people on the dock are here to wish us luck."

Edward too wished them luck as Catherine and Chloe came onto the deck. The three of them found a small table near the aft deck that provided a good view in all directions.

As Edward sat, he asked, "What is Hero up to now?"

Catherine pursed her lips. "Speaking to the wine steward, of course."

Chloe said, "Apparently, I will serve nicely as a chaperone for you two."

Catherine smiled. "I apologize for that. Hero's sense of decorum is lacking."

Edward chortled, and before he thought better of it, the words were out of his mouth. "You do not know the half of it."

Catherine gave him a stern look, and Edward changed the subject to their next steps. They watched as the town dwindled into sparse, low buildings and then shifted into pastureland with sheep grazing in the morning sun. Edward suggested they visit chemists in Bonn to see if any of them knew Alfred. He asked Chloe if she recalled the names of the chemicals Davet was working with. She admitted she was not sure, because Davet had her use codes in the notes.

She said, "He used the code Ng, and also used codes Co, Ce, and Si. He mixed the Ng with each of these and combinations of these in varying amounts. Si seemed to be the one he had some success with."

"Assuming Ng is what I think it is, I can ask chemists about purchasing glycerin for Alfred and see who has an account for him."

Catherine cocked her head. "And what do you think it is?"

Edward evaded the question. "I have several guesses. In the meantime, there is not much for us to do on the ship but enjoy the time. If you do not mind, I think I will find Hero and the wine steward and see what they are up to."

Catherine said, "It is a bit early in the morning to keep up with him, is it not?"

Edward stared at her blankly. "Perhaps as the day wears on, his tongue will loosen."

Catherine arched one eyebrow. "Good luck. Just make sure it is not your tongue that wags. He is a practiced professional. At least regarding wine."

"Duly noted." Edward stood and made his way to the lounge.

The aft lounge had windows on either side and two at the rear of the ship overlooking the deck, where Catherine and Chloe still sat. Edward could see the back of the paddlewheel churning outside and the trail of water foaming behind them. Above the windows were stained-glass transom windows that cast bright-colored patterns on the worn teak floor—a calm, bright display against the fury and noise of the paddlewheel. There were small tables around the room and only a few passengers present. Edward did not find Hero or the wine steward there, so he visited the dining and ballroom, which was surrounded by glass on three sides with a ceiling of smooth wooden beams. The tables had white tablecloths that were bathed in rainbows as the sunshine filtered through the crystal goblets set upon them.

Edward asked one waiter who was setting a table if he'd seen Hero, and he directed him to the steward's office. Edward found Hero and the steward engaged in a lively debate.

"I am sorry to interrupt. I was wondering if you and I could spend some time in the men's lounge, Hero."

"Of course! We were finishing our discussion of the merits of using Scuppernong grape vines to combat the blight." He turned to the steward. "I appreciate your point of view and look forward to perusing your wine list this evening."

Edward and Hero left for the men's lounge, which was a dark room with no windows, only small portholes, and navy-blue carpeting and plush chairs. They sat at a table near the fireplace, and before Hero could call for a wine list, Edward asked for a list of their whiskey selection. *Two can play at this game.*

"I would love to share some whiskey with you. If you are game, of course."

Hero nodded, and Edward ordered two glasses of Glenturret. "We will start our tour in Scotland." As they took their first sips, Edward remarked on the complexity of flavors and gave Hero some history of the distillery. He steered the conversation as they sipped from various glasses from Kilbeggan Distillery in Ireland, to the George T. Stagg Distillery in the United States. They decided they preferred the Glenturret, and Edward ordered a bottle for them to share. With each glass they toasted, and Edward steered the conversation further from whiskey and topics of the day and closer to friends, acquaintances, family, and their upbringing.

With half of the fresh bottle gone, Edward homed in on his quarry. "I hope you will not share this with Catherine. She has little love for Monsieur Bergeron, but I found him to be a very interesting man. Quite learned. He seemed someone I would have some things in common with, such as a shared love of history."

Hero's tongue was thick in his mouth, as evidenced by the slurred response he gave. "Catherine is not wrong about him. You should pay her more heed."

"Have you spent much time with him?"

"No, but I have met him from time to time."

Edward poured another round and hoped Hero would reveal whatever his relationship with Bergeron was quickly, as he felt the effects of the whiskey turn his own diction to mush. "How did he become so successful? Was he born to it?"

"Oh, no. He is a completely self-made man, from what I understand."

"When I met him, he already seemed to know so much about me. I suppose that is how he can curate his goods and services to those who can afford it though."

"Do not make light of it. He trades in information even more than he trades in goods and services. You would be wise to give him a wide berth. I wish...I mean, we should probably be on our way." He checked his pocket watch. "Oh, my goodness. It is three o'clock. I need to rest before the dinner hour." He tried to stand and gripped the table tightly as he brought himself upright.

Edward walked him to his room, and as Hero went to close the door, Edward said, "I have a question. Do you mind if I come inside for a moment?"

Chapter Twenty Seven

H ero held the door open for Edward to enter and fairly fell into a chair in his room.

Edward closed the door. "I saw you at Bergeron's facility in Nancy. Why was he paying you?"

Hero looked away. "You must be mistaken." He laughed nervously.

"He still owes you one hundred fifty bar."

Hero's eyes widened in fear, and he gripped Edward's hand. "Please do not tell Catherine. It has nothing to do with her or her father's business and is something I am forced to do. It does not impact her."

"I cannot be sure of that without more details, and I do not trust your word at the moment."

Hero's shoulders slumped. "Old wine barrels. I sell him my old wine barrels for half-price. It is highway robbery, but I am compelled to do so for reasons that are nobody else's business."

"What does he want with old wine barrels?"

Hero leaned forward and whispered thickly, his whiskey breath gusting in Edward's face. "Smuggling. Shhhhhhh." He lost his balance and fell sideways on the chair before catching himself.

"He uses your barrels for smuggling? If caught, that could bring you significant trouble."

"I know." Hero put his head in his hands. "I wish I did not have to, but he compels me. There is nothing I can do."

Edward stood and patted Hero's shoulder. Hero stood and headed toward his room. Edward strolled the deck to clear his head. Near the dining room door, he saw the man who had been following them in Nancy. The man motioned toward Edward then walked to the deck closest to the paddlewheel. Edward trailed behind. His anger helped him ward off the drunkenness that was stalking him.

As the man turned to face him, Edward fairly shouted, "Who are you, and why are you following us?"

The man had high cheekbones and rather large, close-set eyes that turned down at the edges, giving him a look that resembled a puppy. His sandy-brown hair was closely cropped above his collar, and his clothes were nondescript, in a bland gray that matched the cobblestones on most streets. Overall, he was probably the most forgettable man Edward had ever seen.

"I am sent by Monsieur le Marchal."

"Why?"

He whispered, "To assist you in finding the murderer. My name is Phillipe Vardell. I am a Presbyterian minister here in Bonn. I know that you are Henri's friends Edward Tyrington, sent to investigate his murder by his mother."

Edward asked, "How do you know all this? Who are you really?"

"I truly am a Presbyterian minister. However, I also minister to some poor souls stuck on the French side of the border. Despite the law requiring French citizens to be Catholic, they still practice as Presbyterians. The price I pay for the government looking the other way is to assist the government from time to time, including Monsieur le Marchal."

"That hardly makes sense. Why would the French allow you to minister to non-Catholics? It seems to me they would kill nonbelievers."

"They are not as bad as that. There is some...utility...in having people near the border generally happy and not trying to court the Prussians into freeing them from France. Napoleon would prefer to avoid the type of uprising the citizens of Schleswig-Holstein are creating now on the Prussian border with Denmark. I help keep the peace and can minister to my flock. Occasionally I am asked to perform a task. Usually nothing too difficult or dangerous. This time has been different."

"How do you know such things? Why should I believe you?"

"You probably should not believe me, or anyone else. You are digging into something that is much larger than you realize, with far-reaching ramifications." Seeing Edward's incredulous look, he continued, "I work for Alfonse in the border region, monitoring things. As you know, there have been political tensions here in the past few years. Former Prussians who want their government to retake this region. I do not know how the general unrest fits into Messieurs Molyneux and le Marchal's deaths, but I know there are others looking into it."

"Who? What do you suggest we do?"

"I do not know exactly, I just know that I encountered a few people in Nancy who were also looking into it—people with connections to the Danish prince. Tread carefully. I will help all I can, but for right now, you should be discreet. I will contact you as needed." He turned and walked away from Edward, descended the stairs to the lower deck, and disappeared.

Edward searched the ship and found Catherine in the dining room, having tea. He sat heavily.

"You are drunk," Catherine said.

"Shhhh. Yes, but listen. I met our pursuer. He claims to have been sent by Alfonse to help us and that we are in more danger than we realize."

"He is on the ship?"

"Yes, I met him on deck. I will share more later, but please be careful."

"All right." Catherine turned her head away from his whispers. "You reek of whiskey. Why are you drunk at four o'clock?"

"Hero. But it was useful. I discovered his secret. It does not involve you."

"I am delighted. Now go to your room. You are not fit for company."

As he made his way to his room, the air felt heavy with rain. Edward could see the far-off clouds that washed the nearby fields in gray watercolors, and he watched the storm advance toward the ship. As he stared across the deck at the charging storm, he noticed Chloe speaking to a man. He was sure it was her, in her bottle-green dress. The man was tall, with nearly white blond hair, a face that was almost as pale, and strong cheekbones. He seemed wiry but his broad shoulders gave him a rather imposing appearance.

Edward decided he was too drunk to speak to anyone and went to his room, where he told Davis not to disturb him, even for dinner. He slept fitfully through the evening, awakened by the sound of thunder and lashing rain, and finally falling into a deep sleep after midnight when the storm subsided.

In the darkness before dawn, there was an explosion.

CHAPTER TWENTY EIGHT

E dward sat up and immediately fell off the bed as the boat listed port, then starboard, then settled on a tilt toward the stern.

"Davis!" he called as he pulled his face from the carpet pile.

"Here, sir."

Edward stood and lurched forward to open the door to his cabin.

Catherine came out of her room in her dressing gown and bare feet. "What happened?"

The hallway filled with acrid smoke that burned his nose and eyes. Edward took her hand and ran toward the bow of the ship. At the stairs he turned to see Catherine's maid Daniella and Davis hastening along, and Hero and his man behind them. Catherine grabbed Daniella's hand, and Daniella grabbed Davis's.

At that moment the pounding of his head caught Edward for one brief second and forced him to recall all the whiskey he had drunk. He swayed, whether from the motion of the listing ship or the fact that he was still somewhat drunk, he wasn't sure. Cabin doors flew open as others left their rooms, and soon the smoky corridor filled with shouting people, some in quite a state of undress. Edward climbed the stairs coughing, his lungs burning and his eyes stinging from the smoke.

They burst through the door to the deck amidst a swarm of coughing people. Smoke shrouded the boat, and the deck was full of screaming passengers. Sailors along the rails were attempting to lower lifeboats, but all was chaos.

Edward looked toward the stern of the ship, which was significantly lower than the bow, although exactly where it sat in the water was impossible to make out with the smoke. There was an orange glow and thick smoke billowing from a gaping hole where the deck had previously been above the engine compartment. People were in the water screaming, and others were on deck fighting over life preservers. Edward saw several bodies floating, no movement, as he scanned toward the shore. There were a few farmhouses nearby; already lamps were lit, and people on the shore were shouting and running for the nearest dock.

A sailor was preparing a lifeboat nearby, and Edward fairly threw himself and Catherine toward it. Before it was ready, Edward swept Catherine off her feet and hoisted her into the boat. He shouted, "I will meet you onshore!" She begged him to stay safe. As other women boarded the boat, she reached for his face and kissed him as forcefully as anyone had ever kissed him, her tongue seeking his own in desperation for one last taste. Edward gripped her tightly until the boat's position made continuing impossible. He yelled over the rail his promise to meet her on shore.

He turned to Davis, who had helped Daniella onto another boat, and yelled "Follow me!" He ran toward midships against the crowd of people running from the rising water, like a salmon headed upstream. Edward and Davis pushed their way to the rail and jumped.

The cold water was shocking as Edward plunged below the surface. It felt as if someone had punched him right between the eyes. He resisted the instinct to inhale and swam as hard as he could underwater. As he came up, other passengers fell on top of him, shoving him further below the surface. He pushed them away and swam further from the boat. Another pair of feet drove into his legs and pushed him down again. His lungs burned as he swam harder for the surface. There were arms and legs clawing and kicking at him as he, too, struggled. He finally pulled himself up and his mouth broke the surface long enough to take one gulping breath before he plunged down again. Hands grabbed at his chest and legs kicked him as he tried to get away. He managed another breath before a woman's bare feet kicked him in the head as she jumped from the boat. He dove deep and swam below the chaos to get away from the crowd.

Finally clear of all those who would drown him, he treaded water and called for Davis. He did not answer. He turned around and back again, whipping his head to scan for him. He scanned the ship, whose bow rose into the night like a twisted, burning steeple.

Those still on board shrieked as the boat shifted and their feet flew out from under them. Many fell and slid into the churning, sinking hell that was the midship as it sank. For those holding the rails, it would only be a moment more before they joined them.

Edward swam as hard as he could as the ship slipped below the surface. Edward saw the red and green lanterns waving on the bow of another ship approaching, presumably guiding that ship closer to those in the water to rescue them. He continued to swim and tread water and shout for Davis, but all was screaming and chaos.

Then he heard "Edward!" He spun around at the sound of Catherine's voice but saw no boat nearby.

"Catherine?"

"Here!"

He saw her hand flail out of the water. He swam to her and grabbed her waist, helping to lift her out of the water as he kicked. "Where is the lifeboat?"

"Capsized. Too many people." She sank into the water and came up sputtering. Panicked, she grabbed Edward's head and tried to climb his body as if he were a tree. Edward went below the surface again, his numb fingers trying to pry her hands off his head and neck as she slipped and clung tighter. Her right thumb pushed against his eyeball, and he felt the fire in his lungs as he ran out of air. Catherine was flailing wildly, and she pushed and kicked at him as she tried to save herself each time he loosened her grip. He pushed out the last of his breath, gripped her wrists, and threw her off him. As she flailed nearby, he swam up behind her and rolled her onto her back. Then he snaked his arm over her arm and under her neck, and held her other arm to keep her from grabbing him again.

"Stay calm. I have you." He repeated this over and over until she truly heard it.

She struggled for another half-minute, which felt like an eternity, before she exhaled and stilled herself. When she seemed settled, he kicked as fast as he could toward shore, his left hand side-stroking them forward. She kicked alongside him, but when he stopped to catch his breath for a moment, he noticed her shivering lips were blue.

Edward lied and said, "We are almost to shore." And he began swimming again. A man tried to grab them, and Edward pushed him away. If he got hold of Edward, he'd drown all three of them.

Chapter Twenty Nine

As they finally neared shore, Edward called out for Davis several more times, but there was no response. Edward's feet and hands were numb, and his head was aching with the cold. Catherine called for Hero, but again there was no response.

"Save your breath," Edward said. "They may already be on shore. I am watching for them." Edward swam harder, knowing she did not believe him.

The second paddlewheel ship loomed closer. Too close. Too fast. It had no time to stop before it was in the thick of the swimmers.

Edward yelled, "Kick now!"

Catherine looked at the ship and kicked like a woman possessed. They made the shore just as the moving ship tried to reverse engines and stop. The paddlewheel ran over several people, and the screaming of the crowd in the water intensified as they scrambled harder to get out of the way. Several people clung to the paddles on the wheel, only to fall from the top and be crushed beneath the still-moving wheel.

Catherine and Edward reached the shore, their nightclothes soaked. Edward pushed the hair from Catherine's face. Their eyes locked for a moment before she clung to him, kissing him. He pulled her tight and kissed her back. Their bedclothes sticking together, he felt how small her body was as he held her, his hands smoothing her hair and pulling her close with all his might. She kissed him as a drowning woman breathes air, as if each gulp could be her last. She pulled away for a moment only to return, her tongue searching for his like a life raft, as if only these kisses could save her—or him. He kissed her back hard, knowing he would likely never get this chance again to show her he truly loved her, wanted her to be his. He needed her in his life, for the rest of his life, and that need consumed him with each kiss, each stroke of her hair, each heavy breath. She was the only thing that made his world right. There was no more pretending he could live without her, no more pretending he did not miss her when she was away, or that he was fine on his own. He was not. He needed her, and almost losing her to the damned Moselle River was the moment that proved it once and for all.

When their lips finally separated, Edward mumbled: "Thank God...Thank God...Thank God." His heart and soul were so full of gratitude, he felt he would break. He held back his tears, but his breath came in swelling sobs. He knew in that moment he did not want to live in a world that did not have Catherine in it, even if she refused him, even if she destroyed him.

Catherine clung to him. Tilting her head on his chest, her eyes showed a mix of fear, admiration—and did he dare believe it?—love. Her lips parted again, every fiber of her being imploring him to kiss her. He obliged, his hand cradling her cheek in the softest of caresses.

Someone behind Catherine placed a blanket across her shoulders. He wrapped his arms and the blanket around Catherine and held her as she shook from the frosty night air and the shock.

As he held her, he looked over her head to scan the crowd for Chloe, Davis, Hero, and Daniella. Villagers had brought as many lamps as they could find to help the survivors look for their friends and family. The chaos had settled to a dull roar of names being called and the sobs of those suddenly in mourning. A man in a uniform was shouting orders to the crowd, trying to establish order. He asked people to form lines in front of his officers, who would take people's names and try to reunite families. There were four lines, and Edward and Catherine joined one of them, still wrapped in each other's arms. The ship that had arrived lowered life boats to those in the water and rescue operations commenced, even though that same ship had made the situation worse. Several fishing boats from nearby farms were also saving swimmers. The smoke was clearing, and the scene that was revealed shocked Edward. Their ship had sunk almost her entire length, but a small bit of the bow stuck defiantly from the water, with a small crowd upon it. A fishing boat was approaching to help those still on the riverboat to shore.

When they reached the head of the line, Edward gave his and Catherine's names and asked if Hero, Daniella and Reed had been located or if their names were on his list. The officer did not have their names. Edward and Catherine walked away, and together they scanned the crowd, shouting their companions' names. It was not long before the worry over their comrades outweighed the joy and pleasure of holding one another, and Catherine suggested they separate to search the crowd more efficiently, both agreeing to meet back at the dock if they found someone.

Edward watched as Catherine wandered downstream, wrapped in the blanket, before moving upstream himself. He called for their lost companions. No one answered. Everyone in the crowd on the shore called a different name: Gertrude, Rachel, Amanda, Matthew, Gabriel, the list went on and on. Loved ones of all kinds. Edward had to focus on his own task and push away the heartbreak surrounding him as townsfolk carried bodies from the water.

His mind filled with memories of Davis. How he had comforted him after his father's death and stood by him as his life and finances fell apart, and Edward had to fire all the help but him. Davis had understood how hard firing everyone was for Edward. He'd stayed with him for reduced pay even as he refused positions offered by his father's friends. Edward believed Davis's respect for his father was the main reason he stood by him through poverty. He saw a man's bow tie floating in the water and thought of all the times Davis had tied his for him. Edward called his name again and heard the desperation in his own voice, the panic that shook his normal timber into a soprano's range. He screamed for Davis again, but still no one answered.

As he screamed, Phillipe Vardell took his arm. "Who can I help you find?"

Edward took a deep breath and pushed the wet hair back from his brow. "I am looking for my man, Davis and two women named Chloe and Daniella, and another gentleman named Hero."

"Come with me. I am so glad you are both all right. I saw Miss Briggs earlier." He led Edward through the crowd to a barn.

There were cots in the rough-hewn wood structure for the injured and dead. There, in the midst of it all, was Davis attending to the injured. He was wearing a heavy canvas butcher's apron over his clothes, which bore a constellation of brown and red stains. His shirtsleeves were pushed above the elbow, and his calm professional demeanor was clear from across the room as he carefully dressed an injured woman's wound.

Edward nearly cried with joy and ran over to him. "Davis, you are all right."

Davis smiled as he continued to work. "Thank God you are all right, sir. I am fine."

"Have you seen Chloe, Daniella, or Hero and Reed?"

"Hero and Reed are here. Hero nearly drowned. Shrapnel from the explosion cut Reed. They should be fine but will need time to recover."

"I will retrieve Catherine and bring her here."

Edward headed to the shore to find Monsieur Vardell guiding Catherine and her maid. Daniella was shivering, so Catherine had wrapped her in the blanket she had and was rubbing her hands. They were chatting, and Edward saw Catherine briefly smile.

"I found Hero, Reed and Davis. All are alive, although Hero has been injured. Come with me." Edward walked the two women back to the makeshift infirmary. The chilly night air blew the panicked voices of the injured and the medics around. He heard snippets of questions about where there was pain, or someone asking for more towels to stanch some bleeding, or the sobs of those with their dead relatives. It was a cacophony of grief and confusion. Edward found someone passing out cups of hot tea and took two for Catherine and Daniella.

They sipped their tea as they walked back to Davis. As Edward looked around, the shock of the moment reminded him of his father's death. Specifically, of his violin, which now sat at the bottom of the river. It was a silly thing to fret over, considering the loss of life around him, yet, his violin had always been a source of comfort in the most trying times. Edward sighed and pushed the thought from his mind. It was only a box of wood, after all, especially since the one lost was his travelling violin, not his Stradivarius. Still, it seemed easier to focus on that than to grasp the suffering around him.

When they reached Davis, Catherine straightened her shoulders and asked, "How can I help."

Davis smiled at her. "Could you distribute blankets to those who need them?"

"I can, but if you need someone to help evaluate the priority of care, I am capable of that as well."

"You are very brave, Miss Briggs. If you are comfortable with that, it would be a great help."

Edward looked at her matted loose hair, her dressing gown that was still soaked and clinging to her, and her bare feet, and he gently took her hand. "You need rest. I would hate for you to catch a fever by working after all you have been through."

Catherine looked exhausted, but she shot him a look of earnest determination, and he knew she could never sit idle through such a situation. He found another blanket and wrapped it around her shoulders. He then found a pencil and paper and worked alongside her to prioritize those who needed care. Eventually they had most of the remaining passengers grouped by the severity of their wounds. Despite interviewing many passengers, they never found Chloe.

"Do you think we should check the makeshift morgue for Chloe?" Catherine asked.

"No," Edward said, "I should check. You should rest and drink a hot cup of tea. I will let you know what I find."

CHAPTER THIRTY

Monsieur Vardell was on the morgue side of the makeshift emergency facilities to walk survivors who were looking for their relatives through the aisles of covered bodies. Edward asked if he had seen Chloe, but he was not sure, as he had never gotten a good look at her. He unveiled each face for Edward to see. Some of the dead were corpulent, many were children. It broke his heart to see so many small bodies.

In the second to last row, Vardell pulled back the sheet to unveil Chloe. Her eyes were closed, and her matted, wet hair clung to the sides of her face and her dress. Unlike most, she wore a blue dress rather than nightclothes. Edward sighed and silently prayed for her soul. As he gazed at her, he noticed three purple bruises on the left side of her neck and one bruise on the right. He instinctively put his hand on her neck.

Vardell asked, "What are you doing?"

Edward pulled his hand back. Without a word, he crossed the room to where Davis was working and pulled him aside. "Miss Bellon is among the dead, but I believe she was murdered." He pointed to where her body lay. Davis walked to her and pulled back the sheet.

"Strangled," Edward said.

Davis confirmed Edward's suspicion with a nod and returned to his work with the injured. "There is nothing I can do to help her."

Edward mused over who might want Chloe dead, but could come up with no suspects. He walked to the river and scanned the water again. There were no bodies left to be recovered, and no one remained swimming. He sighed. *She was so young.* He listened to the water rush past as the sky grew lighter. So many had died since the start of this: Henri, Davet, and now Chloe, and no one knew if Evaline was still alive or not. *There is more afoot than I can discuss at the moment*: Monsieur Vardell's words rang around his head like a church bell. Whoever had killed Henri and Davet would not hesitate to kill Catherine or himself.

He saw a doll floating on the water, held aloft by its voluminous ball gown. He reached down and picked it up. He wondered about the girl who owned the doll. Had she survived? Was she a child he had just seen in the morgue area? He put the doll in his pocket.

By the sound of the locals, they were somewhere well inside Prussia. He was uncomfortable being in Prussia, more so than other countries. He could not speak the language, which was true during his time in Egypt too. However, he knew the locals here hated the English and the French. Prussia felt inhospitable. He bristled at the thought of being here. Alfonse had spies who could investigate Henri's death Why not ask Monsieur Vardell who already works as some kind of spy? Why let Edward continue to flail? Now Chloe was dead, and whatever knowledge she had about Davet's experiments was lost. He did not know how to proceed. He did not know how to find Alfred. His skills as an investigator were nonexistent. This was not a role he could succeed at, as much as he wanted to avenge Henri. Others were far more suited to the task. And he could not lose Catherine. If she died on this errand of folly, he would never forgive himself. But as much as he wanted to give up, he knew Catherine would never let him, nor Davis. He just hoped neither he nor Catherine ended up like Henri.

He handed the doll to a man who was taking down the names of the survivors, then went to tell Catherine that Chloe had been murdered. He found her speaking with Monsieur Vardell, and he informed them both of Chloe's strangulation.

Catherine reached for Edward's arm to steady her. "Murdered? But why?"

Monsieur Vardell whispered, "She was the one person who possibly knew the secret Davet was working on. I question whether it was murder, though. How many times were you grabbed as you tried to swim to shore?"

The hazy vision of Chloe speaking to the pale stranger flashed in his mind. "She was speaking to someone on the boat. I saw them as I returned to my room after seeing you at tea, Catherine. He was very pale with white-blond hair." Edward spun his head this way and that, looking through the crowd. "I did not see him in the morgue, nor do I see him here. He was very striking in his features, and tall. Did either of you see such a man?"

"I believe so," Catherine said. "John Reilly. Lovely fellow from Aberdeen. We met him at tea, and he regaled us with stories of his work as a diamond merchant. He is a stakeholder in the Kimberley mine in South Africa and has some fascinating tales about the discoveries there. He is here visiting family and was happy to hear us speaking English. We very much enjoyed his company. Surely you do not think he had anything to do with this."

"Chloe seemed quite relaxed when I saw her speaking to him, which seems unlikely for someone she had just met. It is also counter to how she responded to us when we met her."

"Well, we were skulking outside her apartment."

"Regardless, whoever he was, he may have had a hand in this."

"I will see if I can find more information on this man from the ship's staff," said Vardell. "In case I do not see you again, you will find me at the Presbyterian church near the university in Bonn. Send a note to suggest a meeting. I would rather not be seen speaking with you there. It is too dangerous."

As the sky glowed gray and then red with morning light, most of those who could travel went to the nearest town in farm carts driven by the locals and very few people remained. The dead were left for the priests and the police, while those too injured to travel went to nearby houses. Hero and Reed went to a nearby vineyard, which seemed appropriate for Hero. Eventually Edward, Catherine, Davis, and Daniella traveled in one of the farm carts to an inn in the next town to rest.

The rising sun glinted off the farmhouse windows as they drove and turned an errant cloud purple as it traversed the horizon. Catherine immediately fell asleep, her head resting against the side of the cart. Her face was at peace, all the trappings of society—the makeup, the perfect hair, the shapely clothing—were all gone. Only the essence of Catherine remained, and despite the mussed hair and lack of makeup and finery, or maybe because of it, she was even more beautiful. Edward exhaled and willed himself to stay awake to witness her beauty despite his bone-deep exhaustion. When the four of them arrived at the inn, he touched her arm and gently awakened her. She started and looked around in confusion until she remembered.

The inn was a plain, mud-colored building with a small sign over the door and a stable in the back. Had this been a normal day, he probably would not have noticed this place, and he certainly would never have considered staying here, but this was not a normal day, and Edward was ready to sleep in a barn if he had to.

As they walked to their separate rooms, Catherine fretted about her lost possessions. Edward was grateful he had not brought his Stradivarius violin on the journey. He tried to calm Catherine's growing alarm as she listed off the items that were now sitting at the bottom of the river.

"They will have to remove the wreckage from the river. Perhaps they can recover some of our items." Catherine continued to panic in hushed tones at the entrance to her room.

Edward took her into his arms and whispered in her ear. "We survived. We can replace everything else."

She buried her head in his chest and wept hard. He knew the shock of not only the explosion but also of interviewing and surveying the injured had caught up to her. Nothing he could say or do would make any of that all right.

He held her, rocking back and forth. "You helped save lives today."

As she continued to sob, it reminded him of the night he met her in Egypt, when she sobbed over Dupont's lifeless body. In the finery she wore that night to the pasha's ball, she seemed to be the exact opposite of the waterlogged waif in his arms. So much had happened between them since then. His esteem of her had changed from thinking she was a frivolous, wealthy girl to knowing her to be one of the strongest, most resourceful women he had ever met. With time she would be all right.

Despite feeling sorry for her, he enjoyed comforting her. It broke his heart that only in the most extreme moments did she allow him this luxury, but he resolved to change that. For now, they were alive. She was in his arms, and that was all that mattered.

When she calmed down, Edward sent Catherine to bed and fell into his own bed in the neighboring room. He slipped into sleep only to be startled awake repeatedly by the memory of calls for help, or of faces disfigured and bleeding from shrapnel wounds. He dreamed of watching a dead hand slipping from a floating piece of wood and awoke in a panic to the smell of the acrid smoke that was still in his nose and hair.

A knock on his door awoke him to the blackness of his room. Disoriented, he held his breath, waiting to hear the sound again. He must have slept, but he did not recall falling asleep. The knock came again.

"Just a moment." Stumbling to the chair, he donned a robe and opened the door.

Davis stood with a tray of food. "It is Thursday afternoon. You should eat something."

Edward rubbed his eyes. "Thursday? That cannot be right."

"It is." He set the tray of food down. "Both you and Miss Briggs have received an invitation to Bonn via an overnight train, which leaves in two and a half hours. I have already made preparations, and Hero will follow in a few days when he has recovered."

Edward sat at the desk. The beef soup warmed him, and he realized how hungry he was. "Invited to Bonn—I do not understand. The steamer company is paying our way there, correct? I would hardly call that an invitation."

Davis handed him a telegram. "No, here is the invitation. I assume this is the same telegram Miss Briggs received."

Edward opened the telegram:

Mr. Tyrington—

After your terrible ordeal, we wish to invite you to Poppelsdorf Palace for an audience with Otto von Bismarck. We have made arrangements for your travel on the eight o'clock train to Bonn. We will meet you at the station in the morning.

Yours Truly,

Karl Heinrich von Boetticher

"Why are we being invited to an audience with Otto von Bismarck?"

"I do not know, but Miss Briggs received a similar invitation."

Edward stood. "I must send a telegram to my brother."

Davis said "Please, eat. Write a telegram, and I will send it. We have little time, and you need to get ready."

Edward hastily scrawled a note explaining their situation to his brother. "I cannot play international emissary, especially with von

Bismarck. We are on the verge of war. I need any guidance my brother can give."

Davis took the note and opened the door to find a man standing with several boxes in one arm, his hand ready to knock. Davis took the boxes and closed the door. "I ordered new clothes, sir." He stowed the clothes next to the trunks that the steamer company had provided and left for the telegraph office.

When Davis returned, he handed Edward his brother's telegram and prepared to leave. The telegram comprised four very obvious words: "Do Not Trust Him."

CHAPTER THIRTY ONE

Edward already knew not to trust von Bismarck. The newspapers had been full of posturing for weeks between the Prussians, the Danish, and the French. Von Bismarck had been threatening the Schleswig-Holstein region of Denmark for months over the new Danish ruler of the area, who was apparently not sympathetic enough to the Prussians in the district. Most felt a Prussian war for control of the area was overdue, held off only by the French threat of involvement, which gave the Prussians pause. Edward knew he had no business discussing anything with von Bismarck during these times. He only hoped the British attaché would also be present to prevent him from any grievous missteps.

Edward, Catherine, Davis and Daniella arrived at the station to find it eerily quiet—far too quiet for an imminent train departure. The ticket windows were closed, but a train stood at the platform with conductors stationed at the entrances. It was a short train with only eight cars. There was no one else on the platform except their group of four. Davis approached a conductor to inquire about boarding the train. They spoke for a few moments, then Davis returned.

"We are in the third car."

Edward looked incredulous. "Third class? You must be joking."

"No, sir, the third car. We are in a private car with two sleeping sections. Miss Briggs is in the fifth car. The dining car is between them. This is someone's private train."

Edward and Davis had two sleeping berths in their car. Edward's bed was plush, and there was a small washstand, plus a reading corner with a chair and a lovely window in his room that gave him a view to the east. Beyond Davis's room was a common lounge area with green velvet chairs and a sofa to match, and there were gold leaf patterns on the ceiling. The gaslights lent a warm glow to the room.

Edward sat in a chair by the window. Catherine came from her sleeping coach in a serviceable light-blue walking dress. She had tied her hair back in a bun, and she resembled an elementary school teacher he had in Essex, Miss Kittering. He remembered a day when his father had returned from London early to meet with her. They sent Edward outside to play, but he sneaked below the window and listened. His father lamented Edward's lack of ability with math to the point of calling him a dullard, but Miss Kittering defended Edward even as his father questioned her own abilities as a teacher. She finally cowed his father through a combination of praise for Edward's other abilities and flattery of his parenting. Edward smiled in the private train car. Very few people in his life had defended him, and he wished he had thanked her.

As Catherine crossed the room, she looked at Edward in astonishment. "This is very generous from someone we have never met. Wait until you see the dining car." She sat next to him. "You are smiling. Why?"

Edward looked at the floor. "In that dress, you remind me of someone I once knew."

"They did not have many clothes. There is no need to make fun of me."

"No, you misunderstand. I was not making fun of you at all. She was a significant influence on my life, and I remember her fondly."

Before she could respond, a porter entered the car and informed them they would serve dinner in an hour.

After the porter left, Edward said, "It is very generous, but the most puzzling question is how did they even know we were on the boat? And why invite us? It is all very disconcerting."

The dining car was a study in white and gold: white linens, white walls with gold filigree patterns, utensils with gold handles, gold rims on the crystal goblets, gold napkin holders, white chairs with gold cushions, and gold serving trays stood ready at a station nearby. It was a stunning effect, especially in the gaslights, which only enhanced the golden hue of the room. Edward and Catherine conferred in whispers over dinner regarding what their strategy might be with von Bismarck, but without more information, they were at a loss on how to proceed. Edward wanted to tell her his theory of their invitation, but he knew the walls likely had ears and without more information, his was only a theory anyway, so he kept his conversation to more general terms.

In the morning Edward awoke to brilliant sunlight through the train car window as they raced past farmland then slowed to a stop in a small village. There was a square across from the train station with a large stone church with a spire that rose into the sky. At the edge of the square was a sausage seller. Sausages and other meats hung above the table, and Edward watched him cut and wrap an order for a customer. The vegetable sellers were just putting out their bushels of beets, carrots, and turnips in vibrantly colored displays.

Davis informed him they would arrive in Bonn in a little over an hour as he dressed him. Edward stared at his cuffs as Davis inserted the buttons into his shirt, and a wave of grief hit him and stole his breath. *My father's cufflinks are at the bottom of the river.* The touchstone link to his father was broken, and his heart along with it. Davis inserted the two cufflinks he had purchased. They were onyx and quite handsome, but could never replace his father's.

Davis looked up at Edward and searched his face for a moment. "Do not despair, sir. Your father's cufflinks are in Paris."

"Paris? They were not on the boat?"

"No, sir. Your description of this journey did not warrant such finery, and it is safer to leave such valuables at home."

Edward nearly crumpled as he exhaled. "Thank you for your foresight, Davis. I was sure they were in the river entertaining some fish, and it quite crushed me."

"I am glad to say they are safe, sir."

Edward clapped him on the shoulder, his smile beaming. "Because of your diligence. Thank you, Davis."

The train station in Bonn was large, with four rail lines and three platforms. Stepping off the train, the first thing Edward noticed was the smell of warm bread and savory sausages. It was the perfect counterpoint to the cool windy morning that greeted their arrival. The sun played hide and seek with the clouds, and Edward sorely wanted to buy some food, but their two drivers with carriages whisked the four of them off to the palace.

The town was beautiful, with wide turreted bridges over the river and large buildings constructed in the Bavarian style, with white walls and wooden beams forming patterns on the front. Edward became increasingly nervous about meeting von Bismarck and hoped he would not create an international incident during his visit.

The carriage pulled up to the main entrance of the palace. The façade also had a series of arched windows on the first floor on either side of the main entrance and a mansard roof with windows on the second floor. Edward knew the palace was a favorite summer retreat for von Bismarck, although a portion of the grounds were donated to the local university. He was surprised that von Bismarck had remained here this late in the season; however, it was clear in the reduced number of staff that they were planning on returning to Berlin soon. The palace felt nearly deserted.

The four of them were escorted to their rooms, with Catherine, Daniella, and their escort going to a room on the right side of the hallway, while Edward, Davis, and their escort turned left. Before they separated, Edward's escort said they would have one hour to unpack and change from their traveling clothes before they would meet Herr von Bismarck and would be announced at court. He said that later, they would also dine with von Bismarck. As Edward's mind careened into overdrive at the thought of dining with von Bismarck, Catherine thanked her escort in flawless German. Edward stared at her in wonder, remembering just how rusty his German was.

An hour later, Edward and Catherine were brought to court. The square entrance vestibule had over a dozen gold leaf columns. The vestibule led to a circular gallery which in turn led into the main domed salon next to a garden courtyard. They entered the salon and saw von Bismarck in a chair that, although it was not the throne, commanded the attention of the room regardless. There was a general hubbub of conversation from the large group assembled. As Edward and Catherine were announced, the room quieted. They strode down the aisle toward von Bismarck, and Edward saw some-one standing near the chancellor. *Joelle Le Marchal? What in the world is Joelle doing here?* He opened his mouth to greet her and noticed her almost imperceptibly shake her head.

CHAPTER THIRTY TWO

As they walked toward Joelle, Edward turned to Catherine, whose head nodded ever so slightly, she had seen the sign from Joelle too. He looked at anyone and anything but Joelle. The ceiling was coffered mahogany inlaid in circular and filigree patterns in gold leaf. A large compass rose in black and red granite was the centerpiece of the white marble floor. The afternoon sun glinted off the gold columns and forced Edward to look ahead. Von Bismarck was imminently recognizable, with his large, sandy-brown moustache, bushy eyebrows, and deeply receding hairline. He wore a military uniform that was impeccably pressed and starched, as you would expect from the Minister President of Prussia under King Wilhelm I. Edward studied the naturally stern look on his face and decided it befitted a man with the nickname "the Iron Chancellor." A balding man with razor thin lips, large ears and a powerful jaw flanked the chancellor, opposite Joelle. Another man with thin blond hair and pale blue eyes stood nearby.

Upon hearing the names of the recent arrivals, von Bismarck's face lit up, and a bright, disarming smile crossed his lips.

"Welcome. Thank you for accepting our invitation. I understand you have had a trying journey. Please let the steward know if you require anything. We have tried to anticipate your needs, but if there is anything you lack, please inform him." As he spoke, the thin-lipped man scowled and checked his pocket watch. Von Bismarck said, "Unfortunately, I must attend to a pressing matter, but I look forward to dining with you this evening." Their escort bowed slightly and shuttled Edward and Catherine back to their rooms.

Davis had already unpacked Edward's clothes and stood waiting for him. "They have informed me we are to stay overnight and that you will have dinner with von Bismarck. They have supplied additional clothes for you. Apparently, they understand there were few appropriate clothes to be purchased in Trier. There are several fine options for dinner this evening."

Edward's mind was racing, but he did his best to focus on clothing choices. Davis dressed him for dinner and returned to his own room. Edward paced his room, unsure of what to do next.

He heard a scratch on his door. When he opened it, Catherine scurried in and closed the door behind her. She was dressed in a cornflower-blue gown with a larger, more-old fashioned hoop than was in fashion in Paris these days, but Paris was always setting new trends. He was standing very close to her, and her back was against the door.

"We should assume we are being spied on," she whispered. "Tend to the fire while we speak."

Edward used the poker to scrape away ash from under the grate as Catherine whispered in his ear. The softness of her breath on his ear was ticklish in the most delightful way.

"Why is Joelle here?"

Edward shrugged and put another log on the fire. "I do not know. She was not just at court, but standing *next to* von Bismarck. She is up to something important. I just wish I knew what. I thought she was in Nancy to collect Henri. She should have returned to Paris by now."

This time Catherine shrugged. "We should assume we are being watched and keep a low profile until we know more. I do not know why they invited us here. It is not as if the chancellor wants to discuss shipping with an English company. Far more likely, he has some business with your brother and is using you as an emissary."

Edward sighed and said, "I was hoping you would not say that, but it seems most likely. I am out of my depth in politics. If you see me going astray, please kick me under the table."

Catherine smiled. "I will." Then she took his hand and pulled him up to standing in front of the fire. "We should discuss some other things."

Edward's heart seized, certain of what would come next.

She looked him square in the face. "I should apologize."

His gaze darted to meet hers before returning to the flames.

"As you know," she went on, "I have no wish to court anyone. That being said, our friendship is of a different ilk than any I have previously known. To lose it—to lose you—would devastate me in ways I cannot fathom. I do not wish my actions of last night, when I thought one or both of us might die, to alter our relationship. But I must also acknowledge that my actions cannot help but do exactly that. I do not know where our path leads from here, but I value your friendship above all others."

Edward nodded. "Thank you for explaining. I understand, but I have one question. Do you regret your words or actions? Are there any that would take back, if you could?"

Catherine chewed her lip for a moment and inspected her hands, which twisted a bit of ribbon dangling from her dress. "Was it not enough that I did them...said them? Now you ask more of me. What matters is that I do not intend to act in that way again. Ever."

So there it is. She loves you but will always keep you at arm's length, only ever allowing you to be her friend. He stared into Catherine's eyes, with their dark rings of blue around the grayish blue irises. He wanted to speak his heart, tell her of his love for her, his esteem of her mind, his joy in her company, his desire to have her by his side, but he knew it would only drive her further away. If he had to hold his tongue to keep her in his life, then so be it. He would suffer his desire in silence. He swallowed hard as she turned and closed the door behind her.

Edward lamented not having his violin to calm his nerves, and he grieved that his was at the bottom of the river. He was only thankful that it was his traveling violin that he lost, not his Stradivarius. Still, it was cold comfort. He paced the room, his mind a blur of memories of kisses, questions regarding Joelle's presence, and fear of what von Bismarck wanted from him. After quite some time, he finally focused his mind and settled down to write what little German he remembered, deciding that it might be helpful to understand what others were saying. Even though they would use English when speaking directly to him, they would use German amongst themselves. He drew a line down the center of the page—one side for nouns, the other for verbs—and was filling in the columns when his door opened. Edward turned to see Joelle.

Chapter Thirty Three

J oelle le Marchal pressed her back against Edward's door, similar to what Catherine had done an hour before. Her raven hair was loose, cascading over her shoulders, and she was presenting a scandalous amount of bosom from her low-cut rose-colored gown. The puritanical side of his nature wanted to snatch a doily and cover her up. The more prurient side enjoyed the view and wondered about her in ways he had never considered Henri's younger sister before. It struck him that she should be wearing black, but the thought left him just as quickly as it came.

He stood. "What are you doing here?"

She was noticeably out of breath as she walked to the fireplace and motioned for him to join her there. He obliged, and she said, "It is of utmost importance that you do not know me. I will be introduced as Fraulein Gunter. You must tell Catherine as well. It is of vital importance."

As Edward poured her a glass of sherry, the similarity of Joelle's and Madame le Marchal's voices struck him. Except while Madame's voice spoke in tones of age and whiskey, Joelle's spoke in notes of sultry summer days and even hotter nights that a person wanted to both escape and lazily lounge in. That voice opened many doors, just as summer does, he was sure.

"Of course," he said. "But why are you here?" He stoked the fire to create background noise.

"There is no time to explain it all. The Prussians are up to something, and I need to find out what. Did you see Moltke sitting with von Bismarck? He is the head of general staff for the Prussian military, and by all accounts he is a revamping the military to prepare for war. I do not know why William Nilsson is here. He just arrived this morning, but that is my concern, not yours. The Prussians believe there was a man on your boat, Pieter Haas. Did you meet him?" Edward shook his head as she continued. "He is the head of the Danish resistance in Schleswig-Holstein, and he is now missing. He has white-blond hair, a pale complexion, and sharp cheekbones."

"If it is the same man I am thinking of, Miss Briggs and Miss Bellon, Davet's lab assistant, met him on the ship. He said he was John Reilly from Aberdeen, a diamond merchant. Later I saw him speaking alone with Miss Bellon. We found her body after the ship sank. It appeared someone strangled her."

"Good God. Did anyone know she was Davet's assistant?"

"Not to my knowledge. Just Miss Briggs and myself."

"Did she tell you anything about his work?"

"She claimed to not know what he was experimenting with."

"Share none of this with anyone else. Do you understand?" There was a knock on the door, and Joelle's eyes widened. "They cannot find me here."

Edward called, "Who is it?"

"It is Davis, sir. It is almost time to dress for dinner."

Joelle relaxed a bit. "I must leave. Do not trust anyone here. You are being watched. I had to go through hell just to come here without being followed."

Edward opened the door and put his finger to his lips to silence Davis. He peeked down the corridor and motioned for Joelle that the hallway was clear and she could leave.

Closing the door, Davis began to speak, but Edward cautioned him with a finger again and brought him to the fireplace, which he stoked as he summarized all Joelle had told him. Davis did not recall hearing the name Pieter Haas or John Reilly, but he did not know most of the names of those he had treated or the dead he had attended to.

Edward went to Catherine's room. When she answered, he pulled her to him and whispered in her ear, "Let them think I am kissing you, if they are watching. Joelle visited me, we cannot know her. We will be introduced. If you cannot be careful about Joelle, avoid dinner, and claim a headache as your excuse."

When the dinner hour arrived, Catherine joined Edward and their escort in the hall. They walked in silence to a relatively small dining room where von Bismarck was already waiting with Joelle.

"Ah, Mr. Tyrington and Miss Briggs, it is a pleasure to greet you properly. Court can be so restrictive. This is Fraulein Gunter."

Edward focused on smiling in a manner that did not betray his anxiety. "It is a pleasure to make your acquaintance, Chancellor, Fraulein Gunter." He noted that von Bismarck did not try to explain who Fraulein Gunter was or why she was joining them for dinner. Or perhaps it was as simple as her being his mistress. Edward did not know.

Catherine bowed her head slightly and said nothing. Servants brought glasses, and von Bismarck commented, "We have the finest champagne from the region. I had hoped your uncle would be with us to enjoy it, Miss Briggs. I am sorry to hear his injuries have detained him."

Catherine smiled and said in her most charming voice, "Thank you for your concern. I am certain he would be sorry to miss meeting you."

The question of why they had been summoned burned on the tip of Edward's tongue, but he knew it would be poor manners to utter it, so he waited, and trusted that the reason would turn up soon enough. They ate oysters, soup, salmon, and duck with several glasses of champagne as conversation darted from Catherine, who was acting as if she knew very little of her father's shipping business, to Edward, who discussed archaeology at length. Joelle said nothing of substance and seemed to only utter vacuous small talk, and only when absolutely necessary. Edward felt as if he were speaking at half speed as he weighed each of his words before saying them aloud.

When the main course of duck arrived, von Bismarck circled around the point of their visit. He asked Edward about his brother's work in the House of Lords, which Edward deflected deftly since

he himself had been working in France for some months. Von
Bismarck tried again, only to be turned away again by Edward's
lack of knowledge of Lord Tyrington's affairs.

Von Bismarck changed tack entirely and expressed his sorrow
for the lives lost on the steamship. "You must know Prussia is
looking into the situation and will punish those responsible."

Edward tilted his head. "Responsible? You believe our ship
was attacked?"

"My officers are still investigating, but there are some in your
government who believe this was a Prussian attack. Despite the
current tide of political tensions, I can assure you that nothing
is further from the truth."

"Why would someone accuse Prussia without proof?"

Von Bismarck sipped his wine. "Perhaps they want to fan the
flames of war between Prussia and France for their own gain.
Perhaps the Austrians are behind it. Or the Prussians who live
in the border regions and want the mother country to liberate
them, or the Dutch, or perhaps the English who can pit their enemies against one another to make their own lives easier. There
are a hundred reasons this false information is being spread.
I invited you here to dispel the falsehoods and let you hear
firsthand that Prussia was not responsible for what happened."

"I am very glad to hear that, but is there no room for an
explanation outside political maneuvering?"

"Such as?"

"Such as mechanical failure. The ship's captain was trying to beat a time record set by another steamship company. Could the sinking not have been an accident due to excessive steam pressure?"

Von Bismarck looked stern as dessert was served. "Of course that is the most likely explanation, and my officers are looking into it. If that is the reason, I will be thrilled. But rumors are already flying, and if that is not the reason, I wanted you both to know that we had nothing to do with this tragedy. And, if I may make a request, I would ask you to convey our lack of involvement to your brother. We prefer to avoid enmity with England. You and Miss Briggs are close to people of significant influence in both England and France to whom I wish to convey our intention of peace. But since you mention it, there was one individual on the ship that we are looking for. Frau Gunter's cousin Pieter Haas. Did you meet him on your journey?"

"I do not recall the name."

Von Bismarck turned to Joelle. "Show him the photograph. This was taken just a few weeks ago."

Joelle removed a photograph of a man and a woman from her chatelaine and handed it to Edward.

He inspected it. "I do not recognize him." Edward gently pushed his foot against Catherine's, hoping she understood not to ask to see the picture.

"We believe he was on your ship but do not know if he disembarked before the sinking. He has not been seen or heard from since."

"Who is he? I mean no offense, but many were lost during the sinking. Does he have some connection to the Prussian military or king?"

Joelle leaned in to von Bismarck, flashing an eye-popping amount of cleavage as she did so, and said, "Forgive me, I should never have imposed my family's need on your very important meeting." Turning to Edward she said, "He is no one of importance, only my cousin."

That Otto von Bismarck would bring the weight of the Prussian military to finding his mistress's cousin was laughable, but Edward and Catherine dutifully acted as if they believed her and steered the subject in a different direction until they said their goodnights.

It was long after midnight, probably closer to dawn, the fireplace cold in the darkness and the moon setting behind the bare trees, that Edward awakened to find Joelle leaning over him, whispering his name.

Chapter Thirty Four

The moonlight reflecting off her bosom nearly blinded him in the surrounding darkness. He blinked madly as he tried to determine what was going on. He opened his mouth to speak, but she covered it with her hand and shook her head. When he nodded, she stood back and handed him his robe. As he donned it, she crossed the room to the fireplace and stirred the ashes, looking for some warmth. He joined her and wrapped a small blanket around her shoulders, as much to protect her from the cold as to protect him from the very welcome and very unexpected sight of her cleavage at such a late hour.

He leaned in and whispered in her ear, "What are you doing here?" Her hair smelled like lavender.

She whispered in his ear. "I needed to speak to you." Her breath tickled ever so slightly, and he forced himself to focus on her very obvious relationship with von Bismarck.

"Why? Fraulein, you seem to have things tied up rather cozily here."

She pursed her lips. "I cannot speak about that, but the man in the picture is the leader of the resistance movement in Schleswig-Holstein. He was carrying information that the Prussians are extremely interested in. He remains missing, but there are reports he may have made it to shore. The Prussians want the information he has and to arrest him. Von Bismarck brought you here to question you about him, but also there is genuine concern the English will view this as an attack by the Prussians. Given your brother's position, von Bismarck wanted to ensure you heard from him that this was not his doing."

"He assumes I believe him?"

"He does not have many options and telling you the Prussians were not involved seemed the best course."

"The woman in the photograph with Haas was Chloe Bellon. I thought she appeared too relaxed when I saw them speaking on the ship."

"When we spoke earlier, you said she was Davet's assistant. Did she know what he discovered?"

"She claimed not to. She said that he worked using a sort of code. I believe he was working to stabilize nitroglycerin for use as a medicine for heart conditions."

"In that case, visit Dr. Pfleger. There has been talk of him at court recently, and he may know something about Alfred and how this ties to Davet." She turned toward the door. "I must go. Do not follow me."

Before Edward could say a word, she was leaving. As the door closed behind her, his mind filled with more questions than answers. *Who is Dr. Pfleger? Why would he know who Alfred is?* Edward returned to bed and lay awake the rest of the night trying to decide between a handful of poor options. Dr. Pfleger, whoever he was, was the only genuine lead he had left.

The following morning during breakfast, Edward and Catherine discussed where they would go next in very general terms. Von Bismarck stopped by to thank them again for their visit and express his condolences on their arduous journey. He told them the staff would take them anywhere in the city they wanted to go, and he would be happy to discuss questions about the sinking that their connections in France or England cared to discuss. The conversation was pleasant, and it was clear von Bismarck was ready to end the interview. Catherine asked about her uncle and was told his injuries would delay him further, but that he would be along in the next day or so.

Davis arranged for a coach to carry the four of them to the Bonn train station. They entered through the front doors then left through a side exit and took a second coach to a hotel on the river, hoping to lose anyone who might follow them. During the journey to the hotel, Edward explained to Catherine the story of Pieter Haas, also known as John Reilly, and that the photograph von Bismarck had shared showed him standing with Chloe.

They arrived at a non-descript hotel that seemed a bit separated from the main part of town. They checked in and Davis and Daniella carried their bags up to their rooms while Catherine told the clerk she was suffering from a severe headache and asked how to find Dr.

Pfleger. The clerk provided the information, and Edward escorted her out to another carriage.

As they drove past a wire office, Edward asked the driver to stop. He jumped out and went inside to send a telegram to his brother. He owed him an explanation—or at least as much of one as he and Catherine had received.

They are looking for P. Haas. He was on the boat, now missing. Also want you to know the accident was not their fault.

He informed the operator where to send a response, should one come, and he returned to the carriage. He asked the driver to drop them off a block away from Dr. Pfleger's office.

As Edward and Catherine rounded the corner, Catherine slowed her pace and tightened her elbow around Edward's escorting arm. "Monsieur Vardell is here, just up ahead."

Edward saw him, in his usual long coat, as he turned back toward them and then faced forward again. His hand was down by his side, but he gave a small wave to indicate they should follow him.

As they came around the corner, they saw Vardell nearing the far end of the block, where he entered a church. Edward and Catherine followed him into the building. It was a Presbyterian church and rather austere, with clear windows and none of the artwork associated with the soaring Catholic cathedrals of Edward's youth. The building appeared to be empty. The pews and altar were plain and uninviting. Despite his lack of faith, Edward loved the panache of a Catholic church, with all the stained-glass, candles, and frescoes.

Phillipe led them to a small staircase leading underground and entered a small room at the bottom of the stairs. After they had joined him, he closed the door.

"Thank you for following me. We have much to discuss. We believe Evaline was kidnapped and is somewhere here in Bonn. One of my operatives heard that a French woman is being held by a group of local ruffians. It may not be her." He paused and shook his head. "We are not sure why they would kidnap her. It makes no sense to me."

Edward said, "It makes sense to me. Miss Bellon said Davet sometimes worked with Evaline. Perhaps the kidnappers thought she was helping him." Edward snapped his fingers. "If they are holding Evaline, perhaps they did not find all of Davet's notes and they are trying to get information from her. They may still try to find the formula he was working on. That is good news. Do you know where this group might be holding her?"

"No. I have several people searching for her. I suggest you keep a low profile, as I am sure von Bismarck's men are still watching you. Given your brother's position, it would be unwise to create an international incident. Where are you staying so I can find you if I need you?"

Edward told him, and he and Catherine agreed to share any information they uncovered with Vardell.

CHAPTER THIRTY FIVE

E dward and Catherine returned to Dr. Pfleger's office. His office had a large lattice window next to the door, which had his
name in fancy gold lettering. When they opened the door, a small
bell chimed, and a man's voice yelled from somewhere in the back
of the building that he would be right with them.

Edward looked around. The shop was small, and one wall was
lined with shelves holding apothecary bottles from floor to ceiling.
Edward scanned the shelves closest to him, and his eyes fell on Dr.
Bodrum's Nervous Restorative. He recalled his trip to Damietta,
where Henri had met him at the train station looking like death
warmed over after a night of drowning his sorrows in a bottle of
whiskey after Dupont's murder. Henri had drunk Dr. Bodrum's
on the train and told Edward he swore by it for the recovery of
overindulgence. At the end of the train ride, Edward was nearly
convinced, as Henri had been whistling as he combed his hair, ready
for what awaited them in Damietta. Henri would have been happy
to see Dr. Pfleger agreed with his assessment of Dr. Bodrum.

He scanned the shelves further, looking for glycerin. There was a
bottle, about half full. The opposite wall contained charts of labeled
skeletons and muscles. There was a handsome mahogany desk with

a small photograph of a woman, whom Edward presumed to be Dr. Pfleger's wife. There was a large curtain blocking the view of the rear of the building; eventually Dr. Pfleger came through this curtain and greeted them.

He was a portly man with beefy red hands and fingers the size of sausages. He wore round glasses and had sparse hair on his head, but his dark bushy moustache was apparently given great care.

Catherine flashed her biggest smile and greeted him in her flawless German, which gave Edward a twinge of jealousy. She continued speaking for some minutes, then she and the doctor both laughed. Dr. Pfleger gave her a bottle of glycerin, which she paid for, and she and Edward left.

Outside, Edward looked at her. "Not now," she said. They walked to a park, and when they were certain they were alone, Catherine finally spoke.

"Alfred Nobel."

"I do not know who that is. What did you tell Dr. Pfleger?"

"That my brother had broken a bottle of glycerin that belonged to someone named Alfred, but I could not remember his last name. I was to pick up a replacement and take it to his house."

"All right. Do you know who Alfred Nobel is?"

Her face took on a stern look with pursed lips and knitted brows as she said, "He makes blasting powders."

"Of course! He and Davet were working on a way to stabilize nitroglycerin—Davet for its use in heart medicine, Alfred for its use in dynamite. I wonder if Davet knew what Alfred was doing. Do you understand the military implications of this? If they could stabilize dynamite, they could use it as a weapon. It would make Prussia the most powerful country in Europe. No one else has this technology."

"I am sure Davet did not know of Alfred's true intentions. He would never have worked on a project like that. Now Henri's family has lost France an incredible military advantage to the Prussians. No wonder Madame le Marchal did not trust the government to investigate. They will hang their family as traitors."

"You realize we are the only ones who can clear the le Marchal family. If there *is* a way to clear their names, that is. This is far more dangerous than I realized. You should return to Paris."

Catherine straightened her shoulders. "We have been through this. I am not leaving. I can investigate with you or I can investigate on my own, but I will not return to Paris."

Edward took a softer tone to his voice. "Catherine, your father would murder me if anything happened to you. The most dangerous forces in the Prussian government are involved. You cannot take this risk."

She crossed her arms and stared at him. Finally, she said, "I am not leaving. Besides, of the two of us, only I know where Alfred lives, and it seems we should investigate him."

"If the government did this, what is the point? One of Moltke's operatives probably killed Henri and Davet. I do not see how we can bring the killer or killers to justice."

"Perhaps not, but we are in the unique position to gather information about his work to share with the French and English governments."

"So they can blast each other to smithereens?" Edward said incredulously.

"Yes, or at least threaten to. Then perhaps we can avoid the war that is almost certainly coming. If only Prussia has this knowledge, France and England stand no chance against them."

"That does make sense, as much as I hate to admit it."

After some additional discussion Edward sat and made a list of the things they wanted to investigate and the many questions they had to help them focus. Edward then returned to his room and asked Davis to purchase clothing to help them investigate at night without being as recognizable. He then took a quick nap, anticipating a long night ahead.

Later that evening, he met Catherine in front of their hotel to walk her to dinner. She looked ravishing. Her hair was pulled back with cascading curls surrounding her face. Her dress was violet with cream lace trim, as were her gloves. Edward had chosen a nearby restaurant so they could speak as they walked before dining.

He leaned in and whispered, "We must spend our days and evenings as a touring couple who are here to see the sights, but I have made plans for further investigations after dinner. When you return to your room, there will be a package for you. You will know what to do with it. We will meet at the church two blocks east at ten thirty."

"Oh, this sounds very mysterious. I will do as instructed."

They made a show of visiting the waterfront before stopping at a small restaurant to dine. It was a quaint establishment on the Rhine, with large windows overlooking the river and small tables each with a short vase of dried flowers. Catherine animatedly spoke of her love of Bonn and the architecture as they ate. After dinner, Edward walked arm in arm with her, listening to her as he scanned the area around them for would-be followers.

He eventually saw their pursuer. He was tall and gangly and stood out more than one would want for such secretive work, but he was thankful the man was so easy to spot. He followed them all the way back to their hotel, which they reached at half-past eight.

Once inside the hotel, Catherine and Edward went to their respective rooms to wait for the appointed hour. Edward doused the light in his room and peeked out of the curtains to see if their follower was still about. He was. Edward checked the window regularly, and at quarter to ten, the man finally left.

Davis assisted Edward in changing clothes. At ten o'clock, Edward walked two blocks to the church and waited in the dark near the stairs. It was twenty minutes before Catherine materialized from the gloom.

CHAPTER THIRTY SIX

E dward greeted Catherine quietly. She looked about and, sat-
isfied that no one was near, said, "Apparently Davis has a
misguided view of how thin I am. I had to let the side seams out of
this dress and resew it with added material. Luckily the hotel had
a sewing kit and I am a fast seamstress. If the dress rips during our
escapades tonight, it is not my fault."

"I apologize for Davis's misjudgment."

"Where are we going?"

"Nobel's house."

"What do you hope to accomplish there?"

"I do not know exactly. I would like to speak to him, but that
may not be possible. It depends on whether someone is guarding his
house."

They walked through town a few blocks from the river, frequently checking behind them and doubling back to ensure they were
not being followed. Eventually they were close enough to where
they believed Nobel's house was to walk toward the river. It did not
take long to find the large house with two lions at the end of the
approach. Edward guided Catherine to a copse of trees nearby, and
they waited.

He whispered, "If they are guarding his house, we should see someone walking around." Catherine nodded, and they watched. After twenty minutes, they'd seen no guards. They approached the house and knocked at the door.

A butler answered, and Catherine asked in German to see Herr Nobel.

"He is out at the moment, but should return shortly."

"Can we wait for him?" Catherine said. "We are friends of Davet Molyneux."

The butler had opened his mouth to answer when a woman's voice came from behind him and asked in English, "What are you doing here?" Evaline pushed past the butler. "Come in quickly."

Edward and Catherine followed her into an enormous library filled with books on shelves, books on tables, and books on chairs—piles and piles of books that made navigating the room somewhat treacherous. Edward picked up a book and saw it was a chemistry text. There were three floor-to-ceiling leaded-glass windows across the room, dark as the moonless night. For a split second, Edward thought he saw movement outside. As Catherine cleared books from the green velvet sofa, he scanned the windows but saw nothing further. He dismissed it as a reflection of the warped panes of glass. The butler stoked the fire—rather clumsily, Edward thought.

After the butler had left, Catherine asked, "Evaline, what are you doing here?"

Evaline appeared almost as a twin to Catherine. Her hair had less red and more blond, but they both had blue eyes and high cheekbones and even wore their hair in the same fashionably cascading way. Edward could see the gears of Evaline's mind working as her eyes darted back and forth between them, wondering why they were there.

Catherine took Evaline's hands in her own. She whispered, "We are looking for you and investigating what happened."

Evaline hugged her. "I am so scared, I hardly know what to do." She pulled back, and for the first time, really looked at Catherine. "But why are you dressed in that outfit? And who is this?"

Catherine said "Forgive me, this is Mister Edward Tyrington, a friend of Henri's. Mrs. le Marchal asked us to determine what happened, and we dressed this way to ensure no one followed us. Why are you here?"

Edward interjected, "And we are very sorry for your loss."

Evaline drew a long breath and exhaled audibly. "Thank you. It has been very difficult, and I have scarcely had time to absorb any of it. I just arrived myself and was waiting for Herr Nobel to arrive."

Catherine held Evaline's hand as they sat together on the sofa. "Start at the beginning, and tell us as best you can."

Edward went to the spirits table and poured glasses of sherry as Evaline started her story. "The police told me about Davet sometime around three o'clock in the morning. I was devastated. I knew he had been working on something dangerous, but I did not think it would end this way. My mother ordered the doctor for me, and he prepared a draught for me to drink to help me calm down. I told her I would drink it once I was settled in bed. However, Davet had directed me on what to do in case he was…" She inhaled deeply looked at the floor. "I did as he instructed, and I left."

"But why leave before the funeral?" Catherine asked.

"Davet had implored me that the first thing I had to do if he passed away was inform his solicitor in person. There was some provision in his will that notification by wire was insufficient, and that the solicitor would put certain codicils in motion after notification."

Edward looked at her a long moment. "You did not return though."

"His solicitor is in Paris. Because of his experiments, Davet wanted a counselor who was out of the influence of the university where he worked. Also, several people knew I assisted him occasionally, and it is possible that I, too, was in danger."

"Do you mind telling me what the codicils of his will are? Perhaps there is something useful to be gained in those."

"The solicitor would only share certain aspects with me. Apparently, I was to be kept ignorant of most of what Davet was doing in order to protect me." She gave a nervous giggle at the thought of it and continued, "All I know is that the solicitor sent certain notifications to people he would not identify. There was also some concern regarding whether Davet's death was caused by a lab accident or some other means. How…things had occurred…made a difference to the solicitor's actions."

Edward had hoped for more information, but it was not customary for a woman to be involved in a man's business, so her answer was unsurprising. He simply said, "Thank you."

"After fulfilling Davet's request, I came to warn Herr Nobel that he might also be in danger and seek answers here. When I left Paris, I only knew him as 'Alfred in Bonn.' It has taken me some time to figure out who he was and find his address. I only arrived a short while before you."

They heard the front door open and then a man's voice in the hall. Edward opened the door of the study and stepped into the hall to speak with Herr Nobel without the ladies overhearing.

An older gentleman was doffing his coat as a footman helped him. It struck Edward that the butler was nowhere to be seen. As he opened his mouth to introduce himself, Edward felt a sharp blow to the back of his head, and everything went black.

Chapter Thirty Seven

As he returned to consciousness, the back of Edward's head ached, and his mouth was dry. He thought he opened his eyes, but everything was dark, and he was not sure if he had. His bed felt hard, and his right shoulder was sore. He mumbled for Davis. Perhaps he was feverish again. There was no sound. He put his hand to the back of his head and realized he was not in his bed, but on the floor. He could barely make out the shape of a door ahead of him. The door swam before his eyes, so he closed them and tried again to focus. He did not recognize his surroundings. He slowly pushed himself up to a sitting position and pulled his match safe from his pocket. Lighting one, he could see the stately hall and the door to the study and the scene came flooding back to him: they had found Evaline here at Herr Nobel's house, and then he had been hit in the back of the head. The match burned his fingers, so he shook it out and dropped it.

He stood and lit a gaslight. Signs of struggle were everywhere, from the carpet that was pushed aside as if someone had dragged it across the hall to the broken pottery at the doorway to the study, to the other knickknacks and glasses that had been knocked off the shelves and lay on the floor. Edward's heart swelled with pride. He knew Catherine had fought valiantly, and for the briefest moment, he had hope. She was wily, yet they would assume she was a helpless female. They did not know how crafty and resourceful she could be.

As he looked around, Edward's mind froze on images of what might have happened based on where items were disheveled or broken. It was a play of images that echoed and bounced at the edge of comprehension. He felt he was watching his own mind work, almost as one watches a snow globe: Catherine being grabbed by some unknown man, her trying to fight back. She had thrown a small glass duck knickknack he had noticed from where it stood on a shelf to someone near the door. She had missed, and it shattered on the floor, or perhaps it had simply bounced off the man. He imagined the much more frail Evaline trying to resist but failing. It was as if he had been there, and the pictures of their struggle floated before him, with Edward helpless to do anything but watch. His heart shrank at the thought of what might have become of Catherine.

On the chance that they might still be nearby, he whispered, "Catherine? Evaline?" but there was only silence.

He lit a candelabra and walked through the house. There was smashed pottery near the front door, the shards mottled with blood. Edward suspected they had knocked the ladies out to keep them quiet and easier to move. He knelt down and touched the blood on a shard. It reminded him of holding Catherine as her head bled from a wound in Greece. The tears stung his eyes as they fell and mixed with the blood on the pottery. The house felt still and eerily quiet, and he did his best to pull himself together. He went through the study, then the dining room, living room and lounge, then upstairs to the bedrooms, and finally downstairs to the kitchen and servants' quarters. There was no one else in the house.

He made a second pass, looking for clues. There was nothing to show who the kidnappers were. He found a Prussian cavalry revolver in the bedside drawer in what was likely Herr Nobel's bedroom, but nothing else of note. He took the revolver and tucked it into his belt under his coat, then left to find the local police station.

It was the middle of the night, and only a few officers were on duty. Edward went to the first desk and asked to speak to the officer in charge.

The man behind the desk responded in German.

Edward said "Parlez vous Francais?"

The officer shook his head. "Sprachen sie Deutsch?"

Edward ran his hands through his hair. He tried to remember his German and said something about reporting a crime, although he did not know if the officer understood. The man's expression indicated that he did not. After several attempts, another officer entered the building, and the first one called him over.

Edward said, "I would like to report a kidnapping."

"I am Captain Wallenberger. Who was kidnapped?"

"My fiancé, Miss Catherine Briggs, and her friend, Miss Evaline Molyneux. We were at Herr Nobel's house when someone struck me on the head and knocked me out."

"And who are you?"

"Sir Edward Tyrington of London. My brother is a member of Parliament."

"Why were you at Herr Nobel's house?"

"What difference does it make? I was attacked, and two women were kidnapped."

"By whom?"

"I do not know. The butler let us in. Apparently Miss Molyneux had arrived shortly before and was waiting for Herr Nobel. I heard someone enter the house, and assuming it was Herr Nobel, I went into the hall to have a word with him away from the ladies. I only awoke a few minutes ago to find the house empty."

"Why were you visiting Herr Nobel?"

"What does that have to do with anything?"

"Just answer the question."

"It does not matter! It was regarding a project he was working on. What are you playing at?"

"Herr Nobel's house has been empty for a week. He has left on an extended vacation, and they sent the staff away. Now you tell me the butler is there entertaining guests. Are you sure you have not been drinking? Good Prussian beer can play tricks on an English mind."

"Come to Herr Nobel's house, and you will see."

The officer sighed. "If this is some prank, I will put you in jail for wasting my time."

"Just come."

Wallenberger had a carriage in front of the station and he, Edward, and another officer went to Herr Nobel's. The door was standing open. Edward was not sure if he had closed it properly. Everything was dark, and the officers walked ahead of Edward, who had his gun drawn. They lit the gas lamps as they cleared each room, and after determining that the house was empty, the officers returned to the study and front hall to look for evidence. Edward took a candelabra outside to search for footprints or any other clues regarding where the kidnappers were headed. All he found were some footprints, horse's hoofprints, and carriage wheel tracks that faded to nothing on the hard surface of the driveway.

Edward returned to the officers. Captain Wallenberger asked him, "Do you recall what any of the men looked like?"

"The two footmen looked swarthy, with darker skin and hair, and the butler was bald with clear blue eyes. The man who arrived, whom I assumed was Herr Nobel, was very burly with graying reddish-brown hair and a beard. What will your officers do to investigate and to recover the women?"

Wallenberger looked rather disinterested. "We have done all we can do here. There is nothing identifying who might have kidnapped them. The dark complexions of two of the men might be something to look into. We will ask the other officers if they know of anyone that fits that description in the area."

"That is it? You will ask if anyone knows of a swarthy criminal? An international crime has been committed, and two ladies connected to very influential people in the French and British governments have been kidnapped. I suggest you do more than ask a few people."

Wallenberger moved in close and spoke with a quiet menace directly into Edward's face. "My officers do not have time to chase a problem two foreign women probably got themselves into while on holiday. If you are lucky, I will ask around. Otherwise, this is not worth my time. Herr Nobel and his family are unharmed. That is all that matters."

Edward saw red and opened his mouth to bellow at the man, but thought better of it and said, "We will see about that."

Chapter Thirty Eight

E dward returned to his hotel as the sun was rising, glorious in a clear blue sky. Today was the day Hero was supposed to join them, and Edward was sick to his stomach that he needed to tell both Hero and Catherine's father what had happened. As soon as the wire office opened, Edward was there with a message for John Briggs:

I am sorry to inform you; we were attacked. Someone kidnapped Catherine and Evaline. Any help appreciated.

He returned to his room. The shafts of light through the window that normally would feel cheerful felt piercing and unwelcome, and the cold of his room nipped his fingers. A letter was sitting on the desk. It was a wire from his brother: *No information on P.H.'s location since accident.*

As he read the note, it occurred to him. *I need to see Joelle. She will wonder why I came alone, and hopefully she can help me find some information on where Catherine has been taken or by whom.*

He sent a note to von Bismarck requesting a meeting that morning, and von Bismarck responded agreeing to a brief eleven o'clock meeting. Edward only hoped Joelle was still there.

He arrived to find a much busier court than he had seen the day before. There were far more military men in attendance and almost no ladies. Edward searched the crowd frantically until his eyes fell on Joelle. She stood by a column speaking with some highly decorated officer, her hair in a loose bun that gave her a look as if she had recently left her bed. It was as becoming as it was unrefined, and it was clear the officer was enjoying her company.

Edward turned and made a beeline for her. "Excuse me, Fraulein Gunter, I came to deliver some news that might interest you. Perhaps you could join my meeting with von Bismarck?" Edward knew this was an extremely unusual move, but Joelle played along nicely, and soon she was walking beside him to be announced to von Bismarck.

In a deserted area of the hallway, he said, "Someone kidnapped Catherine and Evaline. We were at Nobel's house."

"What were you doing there?"

"Looking for answers."

They reached the door, and Edward presented his card to be announced. Soon he, Joelle, and von Bismarck were seated in a rather ostentatious study with black granite columns that had gold leaf capitals and windows from floor to ceiling that were at least twenty feet high.

"Thank you for agreeing to see me, Herr von Bismarck. I asked my brother what he knew of Pieter Haas. He informed me that British intelligence does not know of his whereabouts since the ship accident. Also, since he used the word 'accident,' it is unlikely that the government believes the sinking was Prussia's handiwork."

"Thank you, Mister Tyrington, I appreciate you sharing this information. Our sources have also lost any trail regarding Pieter Haas since the sinking. It is likely that he is dead."

"I assumed this would not be news, but I wanted to tell you in the spirit of candor and grace that you showed us the other evening. I also informed my brother that Prussia had nothing to do with our boat sinking and relayed that the ship likely sank because of engine issues, since they were racing to shorten their time enroute."

By the time Edward returned to the hotel, Hero had arrived. Edward went to Hero's room and his heart broke as he said the words, "Catherine and Evaline were kidnapped last night. I am truly sorry. I tried to keep her safe and I...I failed."

"What? What do you mean kidnapped? How?"

"We visited Alfred Nobel's house and found Evaline there. The staff knocked me out and when I came to, everyone was gone. I immediately reported it to the police, but they do not seem particularly interested in finding them."

"Do you have any clues where they might be?"

Edward stared at the floor and shook his head, unwilling to look at the helplessness in Hero's face.

Hero said, "I know some people in the area. I will ask them if they can help."

"That does not sound very promising."

Hero sighed. "That is because it is not."

Edward held the silence like a life preserver, his mind in a fog. Finally he said, "Before you go, you should hear the entire story. Somehow it might be helpful, or perhaps you will see a clue I have missed."

Hero poured them whiskey and stoked the fire. Edward's mind was ablaze, and he shared everything he and Catherine had done, starting with the initial request to find Henri's killer, the time Edward saw Chloe with Pieter Haas on the boat, how he and Catherine had found Joelle as Frau Gunter with von Bismarck, and then later met Phillipe Vardell. He ended the story with the kidnapping. It was a long jumble of words that barely made sense to him, but somehow Hero and Davis seemed to follow it. When he finished, he said, "I do not know what to do."

Hero sat forward. "You should go to Phillipe Vardell's church and tell him what has happened. He may help. Thank you for sharing this. I will contact my friends and see if they can provide any help."

Edward returned to his own room and found Davis waiting for him in his shabbiest clothing. Davis said, "I am going to visit some less than reputable establishments and see if I can get any information about swarthy men and a redhead."

"I appreciate that, but I would prefer if I went with you so you are not alone."

"No offense, sir, but you will not...blend in...at the type of establishment I am thinking of. I will see if Hero's man Reed can join me. He is always interested in exploits in low places. This will

be no different. Besides, he speaks fluent German, which will be a
necessity."

"Thank you, Davis."

After a sleepless night, Davis arrived back at the hotel at first light.
He had found nothing helpful and Edward left to find Phillipe
Vardell. He travelled east, and the sunrise seared his eyes. He shielded
them and hurried toward the church. A few blocks away, he checked
to see if anyone was following him. He did not see anyone, but he
walked a circuitous route for the last few blocks just to check. The
streets were deserted except for the fruit vendors setting up their
stalls along the Rhine.

When he arrived at the church, he found the door unlocked.
The interior was dark, with the only light coming from an army of
votive candles mourning the sick and the dead. Edward reflexively
approached the display, tossed a coin the in the prayer box—which
clattered more loudly than he had intended—and lit a candle. He
bowed his head, and the tears stung his eyes again. *Dear Lord, I am
unworthy of your attention or your help, but Catherine is a precious
soul, and I pray you keep her safe and bring her back to us soon. Please
do not let her be harmed. Do not let her...die.* He wept uncontrollably
then, letting his grief sweep over him in gasping sobs. He knelt in
front of the small candle he had lit. The light wavered in response to
his crying, and he tried to control himself, as if allowing the candle

to expire would have the same effect on Catherine. As he tried to quiet his mind, he felt a presence next to him and looked up to see Phillipe Vardell.

"Mister Tyrington, what is wrong?"

"Miss Briggs has been kidnapped, along with Mrs. Molyneux. I do not know where they are or who has them." He rose and continued, "You must help me find them. You simply must."

"Of course. Where was she last seen?"

Edward explained the circumstances of Catherine's capture and the few measly tidbits of information regarding her captors. He ended with, "Why would they take them? They already stole Davet's notes."

"I can only guess. I would assume they wanted Mrs. Molyneux but took both of them. Either whoever stole her husband's notes found them to be incomplete, or someone else wants those notes and thinks she can give them information about them."

"Apparently Mrs. Molyneux was rather involved in her husband's work. It is possible others knew this."

"I will look into it."

Edward stood. "Seeing if there is information is not good enough. Every minute they have them is another minute they could die." Edward's hand slapped the top of the pew as he continued, "We need to look for Catherine as soon as possible. They could not have gotten far."

"I will see if my contacts have any information. In the meantime, check with the police again. Perhaps they have found something."

Edward went to the hotel to collect Hero and ask him to join him in visiting the police station. Edward was exasperated by the time they reached the station only to find Wallenberger was still on duty.

"I have no information for you yet," he said as the two men entered.

Edward spoke before he could help himself. "Perhaps you could question the man who rents carriages? He might have rented the carriage to the kidnappers."

"Why would they rent a carriage?"

"What if they were not from here? Perhaps they came upriver?"

"When I have someone available, I will send them over to ask him about it."

"When you have someone? When will that be? Two hours from now? Three? Six? She could be dead by then!"

As his fist slammed on the desk to punctuate his last statement, a woman outside the front door screamed.

Chapter Thirty Nine

Several officers raced outside, including Wallenberger. They ran to the left and up the street toward the woman who was still yelling.

As Edward exited the station and reached the street, Joelle took his arm. "Quickly, we must get you out of here. Hero, can you go back to the hotel? I will contact you shortly, but it is better for us to not be seen together."

"Of course," Hero said and turned down a side street.

Joelle removed her arm from Edward's and hustled him into a nearby stairwell. She unlocked the door and led him down a hallway to a second door, which she opened. They entered a courtyard with busts of Beethoven, his father, mother, and several other men evenly spaced around the edge of the green area.

"Where are we?"

"Beethoven's birth house. They have closed for the day, and I am a patron. Stay here for a moment. I need to ensure we are indeed alone." She left him, and after several minutes, returned. "The building is empty. We may speak freely."

Edward's voice rose to a fever pitch as he burst out, "We cannot stay here. There is no time to lose. They could kill Catherine at any moment. We must do something."

The blow she struck across his face caused him to reel back and stung hard. His jaw gaped as he rubbed his cheek and glared at her.

She straightened her sleeve and looked up at him with pursed lips and a sour expression. "Hysteria will not aid our search. Pull yourself together."

"Do you have any leads to follow, Joe—Frau Gunter? Or are we just wasting time here?"

"You are not helping the situation by shrieking at the police. I brought you here to share what we know. I have six people looking for them both. We are doing all we can."

Edward melted then. The knowledge that he was not the only one looking for them, that he and Hero were not alone in fighting an uphill battle to get anyone to take them seriously, calmed him a bit. He sputtered, "Thank you for that." As he sat on a bench, the waves of fear that had driven him abated, and suddenly he felt exhausted and lightheaded. He put his head in his hands just above his knees.

Joelle sat next to him. "I have been visiting Bonn for months. First to establish myself as a widow who moved here, then to establish my connection with court. They required it of us."

"Who required it? I do not understand."

"Napoleon did not simply relax the rules against dissenters to allow them to come back to the National Assembly. There was a price of one type or another for any exiles who wanted to return. For my father to return to his seat, his children had to work as spies for the government, feeding Napoleon information on what other governments are planning. Occasionally we are asked to perform these services for people close to Napoleon."

"Bergeron."

"Exactly. While Henri was investigating Bergeron's request, Davet's work with Nobel became known, and Henri's instructions changed. My father did not want you involved because he had sent Henri to Nancy to recover Davet and his notes—and to remove any connection between our family and Nobel. Obviously it was too late for that."

"I appreciate all of this, but right now, what I need is information on where Catherine might be."

"We believe Pieter Haas, the man in the photograph, has her. He disappeared after your boat sank. It is quite possible he caused the explosion to create a distraction for him to escape. We had men on that boat who were following him. They were lost that night."

"Or the explosion was a ploy to cover up the fact that he strangled Chloe."

Joelle sat next to him. "William Nilsson is von Bismarck's man in Schleswig-Holstein watching Haas and others foment a resistance force against the Prussians. They are on the edge of war now. If Haas gets the information on Davet's work, it will elevate the Danes to a much stronger position, and the war that is coming will be much worse than some short border skirmish."

"What do you know about Haas?"

"Not much more than I have told you. I believe we have found his sister in a small enclave of Sonderborg in Denmark. She is a nun there. I do not know if she supports her brother's activities, but France hopes to keep her and Pieter safe, assuming he is still alive."

Edward tilted his head in confusion. "Why does France give a damn about a nun in Denmark or her brother?"

"As long as Prussia is focused on Denmark, they will not attack France. Also, the better resistance Denmark can mount, the more depleted the Prussians become. France is more than prepared to keep Pieter's sister safe as a mark of goodwill for his activities. Von Bismarck has been scouring the countryside between Bonn and where the boat sank to find Pieter, but has found no sign of him. I only hope he is still alive."

"What do you mean, scouring?"

"Checking train stations, carriage drivers, and hotels in every small town between here and there. He has even had his men speak to the farmers to see if they put up travelers recently."

"Has he checked river boats?"

"Of course, he has even checked boat rental companies, even though those are usually for row boats. He has simply vanished."

Edward considered this news while chewing his lip. The sun cast a strange shadow across the statue of Beethoven's mother. Her features shortened oddly, and he recalled the night of the sinking. The frigid water, the other passengers nearly drowning him, the second paddleboat killing some of those in the water.

Suddenly he sat up straight and stared ahead. "Unless another boat was there to meet him."

"What do you mean?"

"There were several boats who came to the aid of the sinking ship that night. One other river boat made the situation worse by approaching the swimmers too quickly. That boat drowned some of the poor survivors. But that was not the only boat. There were several smaller boats that came along to rescue people. He may have been plucked from the water and taken here—or somewhere else—by his own friends."

"If that is the case, I doubt anyone will find him."

Edward stood. "Thank you, Joelle. I am going to see what I can find out about boats moored in the area. Send word if you find anything."

Joelle walked to the door and unlocked it. "Of course."

Edward returned to his hotel to again collect Hero.

CHAPTER FORTY

E dward found Hero in his room. He had already been drinking, and he waved his glass dangerously as soon as he saw Edward.

"Oh, I feel so privileged to see you after that witch, Joelle, shoved me aside like an unbidden insect. Who does she think she is? I am Catherine's family. Who are you? Just some downtrodden English lord's brother who cannot make a name for himself in governance or anything else."

Edward pushed past him. "I do not have time for your drunk rantings. I have an idea that I need to investigate. It is the only lead we have. You can assist me or not, that is your choice, but I came to invite you. Now that I see what state you are in, perhaps it is best if I go alone." Edward turned toward the door, but Hero blocked him.

"What information do you have?"

Edward related what he knew about Haas and the Dutch resistance, and his idea about the boat. "I need to investigate all the boats moored in the area."

"That is no small undertaking. There must be hundreds."

"Hence my request for your assistance. But if you are unable, I will go it alone."

Hero set down his glass, donned his hat, and opened the door. "Let us go."

They took a carriage to the marina first. There were dozens of boats docked there. Some for the day, others for longer. Those who had the means to travel down or up the Rhine were taking advantage of the beauty of the day.

As Edward surveyed the docks of moored boats, he said, "These boats are flying the Prussian flag at their stern. I should have known it would not be as easy as identifying the Dutch flag. Come, let us start at the dock to the right and work our way across."

They walked past all the boats at the first two docks, just giving them a cursory look. The open-hulled boats were moored in this section, and other than looking for some sign of Haas or Dutch ties, there was little to investigate that was not clearly laid out for all to see. The third dock was a mix of open-hulled boats and those that had a small enclosed cabin. For each cabin boat, Edward knocked on the hull, and if anyone responded, he said he had a friend docked here but did not know where. Then he described Haas. He and Hero saw about half of the owners of boats with cabins. The other half had no one aboard. Edward vowed to himself to come back later if necessary.

While Edward was visiting the last few boats, Hero went to a small commissary for canoe rentals. Edward joined him at the end of the dock, and they rented a craft. After a few halfhearted strokes, Hero set his paddle across his lap and let Edward paddle them upriver. Edward was less than pleased with taking Hero on what he clearly regarded as a pleasure cruise, but that was the least of his problems, so he kept quiet about it. Tall trees, many without leaves, lined the river with their surrounding carpets of oranges, yellows, and reds fading to brown along the banks. Brown leaves floated past them as well, and each pull of the paddle swirled them in circles like the Charybdis of thoughts in Edward's head.

They passed several private docks near the marina, but most were empty. Edward planned to paddle upstream along the east bank then come back along the west bank of the Rhine. The fourth dock had a boat moored, but no one was aboard. They called out to two other cabin boats but received no response.

Hero's attitude quickly became testy. "Why exactly are we on this wild goose chase? Most of these private docks will be for boats that the homeowners have, not for guests mooring there."

"Because we have no other leads, and we are going to follow this one until something better comes along. Unless you would rather I leave you at the nearest dock. It is not as though you are paddling, so it makes no difference to me whether you are here."

Hero picked up his paddle and dipped it a few times before again putting it to rest across his legs and turning to speak to Edward. "The afternoon is hot, and I am not prepared for this level of physical exertion."

"Perhaps if you kept our goal of finding Catherine in your mind, you might find yourself more motivated."

Hero pursed his lips and exhaled sharply before turning back to face upstream. Edward resolutely called out to each boat that had a cabin until they had traveled far enough upstream as to be quite far away from town. They had not seen a boat near this side of the bank for a while. As they approached a bridge, the sun slipped below the horizon, blanketing the world in a grayish blue as a man lit the torches across the bridge.

Edward said, "This looks like the area near Nobel's house. I recognize that bridge and its torches, which you can see from his living room."

Edward looked up at the top of the bluff. He could not see Nobel's house, but farther downstream he saw a boat moored to the dock. The boat was larger than most he had seen on the river, and Edward wondered if this was Nobel's boat.

He whispered to Hero, "Do not make a sound. I want to observe this one." Hero nodded, and Edward steered them past the boat along the opposite shore, then closer to the boat as the current carried them downstream.

The boat was unusual. It was even larger than he had first surmised. The cabin area was at least half of the boat, with small open areas at the fore and aft that were open and contained masts in front and a small cockpit in the rear. Edward steered past silently, letting the current carry them by. When they reached the bow of the boat, as he was considering calling out, he saw in the reflected light from the lanterns on the bridge a small painted crest with fleur-de-lis on the bow. Whose crest was that? He knew he recognized it, but could not place it. They floated on for a few minutes before it occurred to Edward: it was the crest on the signet ring he had found in Henri's apartment. Somehow this boat was linked to Henri, and there was no time to waste in finding out how.

CHAPTER FORTY ONE

E dward quietly made his way farther downriver before putting all his effort into paddling as fast as possible. Hero even helped, and soon they were at the homes behind the Presbyterian church.

Edward instructed Hero as he stopped next to a small dock. "Do you see the church between these houses? I need you to go there and ask for Phillipe Vardell. When you find him, tell him everything that has happened and that we need the police to help investigate this ship. I will take the canoe back to the ship and make sure it does not leave."

Hero jumped out of the boat far more deftly than Edward would have thought, given his size, and ran.

Edward spun the boat around and paddled hard upriver again. His lungs were on fire as he continued to pull the canoe upstream. Soon he made out the shape of the ship in the looming darkness. Someone was lighting the lanterns on the bow and stern. Edward stopped paddling and steered into the sweeping arms of a weeping willow in the hopes of not being noticed.

After a few minutes, the man went below again, and all was silent. Edward slid the canoe closer to the dock within the branches of the willows and other trees along the bank. Once he was in position, he grabbed a handful of branches to keep himself stationary. He could hear people speaking within the boat, but their voices were muffled, and the constant sound of the river lapping on the gunnel of the canoe further drowned out the voices within. He waited. Each beat of his pounding heart counted out more and more time that he was afraid to waste as he waited for Hero and the police.

Edward saw three men climb up on the boat's deck. They seemed to be focused on the other side, and Edward saw the bow of the boat slip further from the dock.

They are preparing to leave. Edward's mind raced. He did not want to lose the boat, nor did he want to approach them without someone—preferably several someones—with him.

As the boat left the dock and started her paddlewheel, Edward's panic decided for him. This was the only clue he had left. Somehow, whoever was on that boat had a connection to Henri. He paddled the canoe toward the boat and grabbed the aft ladder. He hoisted himself onto the bottom rung and let his canoe fall back into the darkness. His slick-soled shoes slipped, but he caught himself. He hooked his arm around the ladder, pulled his shoes off, and held them in his hand. He listened closely for a few minutes, spray from the river soaking his feet and legs, then climbed to the top of the ladder so he could just see the deck.

He was behind the cockpit, where he saw one man steering. At the bow, he saw one other man securing rigging in the low light from the fore lantern. There were windows on the port side of the cabin, but the drawn curtains prevented any view. He crept over the railing, his feet slipping on the deck in his soaked socks, and skulked below the railing toward the aft lantern. He stretched to extinguish the light.

It was a few minutes before the pilot noticed the dark lantern, but when he came out to relight it, Edward hastened to the front of the cockpit and out of sight. The captain bellowed at one of his mates about the mess of water on the floor as Edward slipped into the cabin.

The room was dark and smelled odd—medicinal, but there was a burnt odor as well. It reminded Edward of Davis. He had smelled the burnt odor before, but he could not place it. It was sweet, and it seemed he knew what caused it, but he could not remember.

As they passed the marina, light flooded the room from outside. In the shifting light, Edward saw Pieter Haas on the bed.

He approached the bed, and the cloying burnt smell became stronger. Then he saw it: the pipe, the scraping tool. Opium. That was the smell. In the dim light, he saw a bandage across Haas's chest and another around his left wrist.

Edward said, "Pieter, wake up. I need to speak with you."

He gave no response, and Edward whispered again. Still, he slept. Edward could barely hear his breath. He placed his fingers on his neck. His pulse was slow. *They drugged him.* He tried to sit Pieter up, but he was as limp as a rag doll and only slumped to one side.

The door opened quickly, and the brightness of the lantern the intruder held blinded Edward. When his eyes adjusted, he saw the gun pointed at him.

"Get away from him. Go to that wall and put your hands on it." The instructions were in German, but with a foreign accent. He waved the gun to point Edward toward the far corner of the room. Edward raised his hands, and Pieter slumped down. Edward walked slowly to the corner and faced it.

The man felt Edward's belt for weapons, but Edward had left his gun at the hotel, not even thinking it might be useful until now.

"Who are you and what are you doing in here?" barked the man.

Edward's mind spun, and before he knew what he was saying, words tumbled from his mouth. "Your employer sent me to check on your progress."

"You work for Johann?"

"Yes. Why do you still have him?" he said, pointing to the lump of Pieter Haas slumped on the bed.

"You need to speak to the captain if you are who you say you are."

Edward turned toward him. "Lead the way."

The man shook his head. "No, I will be behind you with the gun." He opened the door and motioned for Edward to go through it. Edward walked toward the stern of the ship.

A voice cried out in the darkness, "Police! Stop this boat."

Edward turned. The man behind him pointed his gun toward the police, and Edward spun and punched him square in the jaw. As the man dropped to the deck, Edward shouted, "They have Pieter Haas on board."

Another mate came at Edward with his gun drawn. Edward ducked back into the cabin and slammed the door. When the man opened it after him, Edward kicked the gun from his hand and punched him, but the blow landed with less force than Edward had hoped, and the man punched him in return. He reeled from the blow, and the man jumped toward him as he twisted out of the way. The man landed on Pieter, who made a sound from the wind being knocked out of him but nothing more. Edward fell across the man's legs and splayed himself on top of him to restrain his arms before cracking his own head into the fighter's, knocking him out. Edward groaned in pain and rolled off the man as Hero ran in.

"Edward, are you all right?"

Edward grunted, "Pieter Haas is here. He is too drugged for questioning."

Hero helped Edward up to his knees, then Edward slowly found his feet and stood.

The police had restrained the three men on the boat. Hero called out to the officers, "We need medical attention for this man immediately."

They tied the captain of the boat to the rail, and one officer steered them toward a small dock, where they quickly tied the boat off.

The police told Edward they were taking the men from the boat into custody and would have a doctor look at Pieter Haas.

"We need to question him," Edward said.

"You and several other people. Come to the police station in the morning."

CHAPTER FORTY TWO

It was midmorning when Edward and Hero arrived at the jail. Edward was not at all sure what his intention was in seeing the police or Haas, but he knew he would figure it out when he got there. When they entered, the station was relatively quiet, with most of the officers out on their assignments.

Captain Wallenberger scowled at him. "What do you want?"

"I came to speak to you regarding the man Haas, whom you captured last evening. I assume you still have the men from the boat in custody; is that correct?"

"No. Von Bismarck's men came and took them about an hour ago. They said they were taking him to the jail at Poppelsdorf Palace."

Edward thanked him and exited the station. Outside, he hailed a carriage.

As they rode, Hero said, "Von Bismarck will not like our arriving at the palace uninvited."

"To hell with him." Edward's nerves were shot. Between that and his worry for Catherine, he did not give a good goddamn about von Bismarck's feelings.

When the carriage arrived at Poppelsdorf Palace, the footmen greeted them and the guard asked, "Are you expected at the palace today?"

"Not expected, but we have business with Herr von Bismarck."

"If you do not have an appointment, he is not receiving visitors today."

Hero stepped in front of Edward and handed the footman next to the guard his calling card. "Would it be possible to see Madame Gunter?"

The footman nodded, and another footman led them to a small waiting room just inside the door. Edward waited a minute after the footman had left, then he reopened the door and peeked down the hall. He saw no one, so he exited the room. Hero whispered, "Edward, no," but Edward ignored him and closed the door. He jogged down the hallway, turning left and right as he remembered from his overnight visit a few days before. He peeked around a corner and saw a guard. Edward walked right past him, and the guard called for him to halt. When he did not, the guard grabbed him.

"Who are you, and what are you doing here?"

Edward stayed silent, and the guard roughly led him down several passages and into the main hall. Von Bismarck sat at the desk where Edward had previously seen him, only this time he was meeting with the French ambassador. People in the gallery gasped as Edward was half dragged up to von Bismarck.

The guard said, "I found this man skulking in the hallway."

Von Bismarck looked incredulous. "Mister Tyrington, what are you doing here? Skulking seems a bit beneath you."

"I need to speak with a prisoner you are holding."

Von Bismarck gave a smirk. "How convenient. Take him to the jail for trespassing."

Edward was not sure how his little ploy was going to end, but he hoped it was the same jail that held Haas.

The guard hauled him to the jail deep in the earth's belly. There were several cells with iron bars and floors of concrete covered with a thin layer of mud from what was likely flood waters in the past. The cells were full of people. Edward was led to the one containing Pieter Haas. How his luck had put him here he did not know, but he was grateful for it, even if he was in a Prussian prison.

Haas lifted his head, saw Edward and said, "You. What are you doing here?"

"Arrested. Same as you."

"For what?"

"Does it matter?"

"Not really, I suppose. Who are you?"

"Edward Tyrington. There is no easy way to say this, so I will come right out with it. I need your help. Someone kidnapped my fiancée and her friend. Some are saying it was likely you. I will move heaven and earth to get her back. You must help me."

Pieter sat up. "You are the reason I am here. I am unlikely to help you at all."

Edward rolled up his sleeve. That morning he had drawn a cross in charcoal on his arm in case he met Pieter so he could explain without words that his sister, a nun, was in danger. Now he rolled up his sleeve to show him the cross. "I had hoped to avoid this, but there are people looking for your sister." He pointed to the cross. "They know who she is and where. Some want to use her to get to you; others, my friends, have the power to keep her safe. How much you help me will determine her safety as well as yours. It is your choice, but you must choose now."

Pieter searched Edward's eyes for the truth of his words, and Edward saw his resolve fade like sunlight at dusk. Pieter moved to sit on the ground and used his finger in the mud to draw a building. A church. He drew other buildings next to it, but they were much smaller.

Edward whispered, "Munster?"

Pieter said, "I don't know for sure. I did not kidnap her, but there are smugglers that operate from the church."

As Edward sighed, he heard a loud crack at the end of the hall, and the guards closest to their cell ran toward the noise. There were three more loud cracks, and then Hero walked up holding keys and a large club that he had apparently taken from a guard. He unlocked the cell door.

"Hurry, they are only unconscious and will wake up any minute."

Hero grabbed Pieter. "Come on. They will kill you here."

As Pieter and Hero ran up the stairs, Edward grabbed the guns of the guards lying on the floor. He followed Hero to the main level, where Joelle was waiting.

"Thank God you are all right," she said.

Edward handed each of them a gun, and Joelle led them through a servant's passage and out the service door near the stables. There was one liveryman and four stableboys congregated near the stable office. The liveryman was reprimanding one boy and smacking his crop against his desk to emphasize his point.

"We should go to the carriage house," Joelle whispered "There are at least two carriages hooked up and ready for people who would leave shortly." She hurried away before Edward could ask her what the plan was.

The three men crept along the outside wall and raced between hay bales to get to the carriage house. No one was about; however, there was only one small carriage harnessed, which was too small for the four of them, even with one driving. The other carriage was unharnessed, but two horses were tied off outside. Edward found tack for one horse, and he and Hero quickly set about saddling it up. Hero then put two sets of tack into the driver's box of the carriage.

Hero untied another horse outside the main stable and whipped it so it ran toward the castle. Edward saw the stable boys run after the horse, and then he saw Joelle dart between hay bales toward them. Hero put Pieter into the carriage, quietly took the carriage out, and drove toward Joelle. She broke into a run, and Hero stopped just long enough for her to jump in. Edward mounted the horse he had saddled and raced after them. They headed west, away from the lake that partially surrounded the palace. As they crested the hill at the edge of the castle grounds, Edward heard a boy yell that the carriage was gone.

He knew it was only a matter of time before someone from the stable came looking, so they scuttled the carriage just past the rise and saddled the two horses. Pieter sat behind Edward, and Joelle and Hero each took a horse. They rode into the woods, keeping away from the road, and turned north toward town. The riding was slow through the forest, but they reached Bonn in decent time. They navigated the woods to find the section closest to the Munster Kirch, which was the large church at the center of town.

As they tied off the horses, Joelle took Hero aside. "Hero, I need you to do me a favor."

Edward knew Joelle was arranging for a way to help Pieter's sister. He kept Pieter occupied by inspecting his injuries so he could not hear Joelle's instructions.

After Hero left on one of the horses, Edward asked, "What was your relationship with Miss Bellon? Was she giving you information?"

"She was selling information on nitroglycerin to the highest bidder. She only agreed to meet me after von Bismarck was unresponsive to her demands.

"Did you murder Miss Bellon?"

"What? Are you sure she was murdered? The boat sinking killed many people. Although, to be honest, someone may have sunk the ship just to eliminate her. People like von Bismarck do not take lightly to being teased with important information for sale. I am sure he did not respond because he felt he had easier methods of gaining the information, like perhaps murdering her and stealing it."

Edward thought back to the marks on her neck. "It appeared someone had strangled her."

"It was not by my hand. But to be honest, she may have been meeting with others on the ship trying to broker a deal. I owe you my life after you rescued me today. I am telling the truth. It was not me."

Edward left him to rest a bit and sat with Joelle, telling her what Pieter had said. Hero returned a short while later, saying he had been successful, and handed Joelle a piece of paper.

Joelle turned to Edward. "As much as I would like to help you, I need to get Pieter to safety. I have a plan and a place to take him for now. Since they have probably figured out my role in your jailbreak, I will not return to Bonn. If you need me, wire Davet's mother in Nancy. I will do what I can from there. Best of luck."

"Thank you for all your help."

Joelle and Pieter took one horse and rode west toward Belgium.

Long after night fell, Edward and Hero approached the church, with only a vague idea of a plan.

CHAPTER FORTY THREE

The large plaza of cobblestones around the church was deserted. The smell of roasting meat wafted across the square from a nearby restaurant and made Edward hungry. He saw the three spires of the cathedral barely outlined against the darkness of the night. The stained-glass windows of the semicircular apse that curved between the two spires shown with a lovely blue and red light. They stood on the east side of the square in semidarkness, watching the few people who were there. Most were on their way somewhere and came in and out of view rather quickly. There was a small bar across the plaza with a few men inside and one man outside who seemed too drunk to know where he was going. He went to the corner then turned around and headed back to the bar. He waited outside as if deliberating whether another drink was really what he needed, and apparently deciding in the negative, left the plaza altogether.

Edward and Hero circled the church once to see where all its doors were located. As they were about to enter the main door, Edward pulled Hero into a corner to confer.

"Where would someone hide a person in a church? So many people come and go; there must be a secret place. What place would be secret within a church?"

"Let us go in and see what it looks like. It cannot hurt to do that. I doubt we would even see anyone, as it is so late," Hero said.

They agreed and went inside. The only light was from the votive candles at the entrance, a series of lanterns along the main aisle, which seemed impossibly long, and two candelabras on either side of the altar. They spread out and quietly made their way to the altar area, hoping the priest would not be awake to greet them. They heard a door open somewhere nearby and voices coming toward them. Without a word, Edward and Hero together ran toward the door and hastily fled the building.

Once outside, Hero insisted they go to the bar across the square. It was small and homey, with honey-colored wood for the bar and the few tables inside, and dark-paneled walls. There were only a few gaslights inside, and the bar felt cozy and inviting. The bartender laughed at them as they entered and spoke to them in German.

Edward asked, "Parlez vous Francais?"

The man smiled and repeated himself in French. "I said, it is many a day that a man comes from church to the bar, but it is rare indeed that they fly as fast as that. What can I pour you?"

Hero said, "Whatever Gewurztraminer you have will be fine for me." Edward asked if the kitchen was still open and was informed they only had a beef stew, which he ordered with a beer. Hero then added, "We only wanted to see the interior of the church. It seems beautiful, but we did not want to, how shall I say, engage in conversation."

"Ah, Father Miller is a fine one. But at this late hour, perhaps it is best to let him rest. He is not as young as he once was. And anyone who knows Father Miller knows that if you start a conversation—well, you'll lose an hour at least. I didn't say I blamed you for rushing."

Edward asked, "I assume there was an ossuary here at one point, is that right?"

"Good God, you're not one of those medical students, are you?"

Edward recoiled slightly. "No, I am an engineer," he lied. "They usually made catacombs from old quarries, and I specialize in mines and quarries."

"Oh. Well, that's a different story then, isn't it? Yeah, there was a quarry. They built most of the city buildings from stone blocks cut there."

"It must have been a massive quarry for all that."

"Yes. Of course, it was all closed down years ago, before I was born even, but the rumor is that the quarry extended all the way to the river. If you are really interested, you can ask Jacob Lehman. His father was the last engineer for the mine, but he died years ago. I'm sure Jacob has some stories though."

Hero smiled. "I bet he does. Did he share any of them with you?"

"No. not really."

After more pleasant conversation, Edward and Hero finished their food, thanked the proprietor and left.

They fell in step and ambled toward the river as they spoke. Edward said, "I will not sleep tonight. I plan to stay here and find a way in."

Hero put his hand on Edward's arm. "It is late. We can look for a secret place inside the church, but clearly there are still people awake in there. We will need to wait a few hours."

A thought started crystallizing in Edward's mind. "If the mine used to ship block via the river, then there may be an opening near the river that leads under the church, which would be the perfect place to hide someone. Besides, we cannot go back to our hotel. It is almost certain that someone is waiting for us there."

"Hopefully they have not detained Reed and Davis."

Edward sighed. "Hopefully."

Hero saw a group of boys standing beneath one of the gas lights and asked Edward if he had a pencil and paper. Edward did and Hero wrote a note and asked one of the boys to run it to the hotel. After one of the boys left, Hero told Edward "I wanted to get a note to Reed."

"What? What if it is intercepted by von Bismarck's men?"

"Years ago we made up a set of code words, so we could communicate without anyone nearby understanding what we were saying. It has proven to be handy many times. I am sure that even if the note is intercepted, it will make no sense to anyone but Reed."

"I am glad of that."

They walked east toward the Rhine. A block from Munster Platz at the edge of the university, there was an enormous statue of an angel on a huge two-story plinth. Edward stopped and looked up at it. It seemed dark and fearsome in the flickering gaslights nearby.

"There are four, are there not?" he asked.

"Yes, this is the eastern one, Gabriel blowing his horn."

"Have you seen the others?"

"Yes, last time I was here for the Riesling festival. Let me see. Michael is west, Raphael is south, and a clock with cherubs is north."

Edward scanned the ground around the statue. "Do you see any doorway or manhole type of opening here?"

Hero looked at the area around his feet. "No. What are you thinking?"

"That one of these might make a perfect entrance."

Hero gestured at the ground. "But there is none."

"You said one has a clock?"

"Yes, the northern statue."

"Let us look there. Someone has to fix the clockworks periodically. That might be our best hope."

"It is certainly better than scrabbling along the riverbank looking for some hole in the ground."

They walked a few blocks north and turned to the west toward the area directly north of the church. A fog was rising off the river, and it lent a gloomy air to the night as each gaslight flickered in its hazy glow. There were fewer people about, and Edward shuddered as the fog chilled him.

They reached the clock statue, and Edward circled the base. On the northern side of the plinth was a small door—tall, but not very wide. Someone Hero's size would have to walk through sideways.

"By the size of the door," he said, "it seems they must have children service the clock."

"It would seem so."

Edward pulled his lockpicks from his pocket. The lock was clean and polished, and had clearly been used recently. Hero kept watch on the square while Edward closed his eyes and focused all his attention on his fingers. He felt the lever inside lift and then drop again. Readjusting his grip, he tried again and lifted the lever while adding a second tool to the lock. With the second tool in, he turned the pick clockwise. The bolt retracted, and he opened the door.

Chapter Forty Four

B y the dim glow of the gaslight across the street, Edward could see a small spiral staircase rising into the clockwork statue of cherubs. He knelt down on the dirty wooden floor and felt with his fingers around the edges, then worked his way inward toward the center of the floor. A quarter of the way in toward the center, his finger caught on an edge. He followed it around until he had outlined a trap door. He then felt within the rectangular outline for a mechanism. Eventually he felt a small metal ring, mostly buried in the dirt. He pulled out his lockpick tool and scraped the floor around the ring.

"There is an entrance to something below us, but it has not been used recently." He continued scraping away the hardened mud until he could pull the ring up and lift the trapdoor just a bit. He peeked through the opening. It was pitch black, but he saw the top of a ladder just below the door. He lifted the door. "I am going down."

"Are you mad? It is black as ink down there. You will be blind. And who knows what is down there?"

Edward stepped onto the top rung of the ladder. "That is just what I intend to find out." Before Hero could protest, he clambered down as quickly as he dared.

He had climbed down about twenty feet when he reached the bottom. He could see Hero's face dimly outlined by the gaslights above. He whispered. "I am at the bottom. I will return soon."

"Wait there for a moment," Hero said before walking away from the trap door. Edward saw the outer door close to allow only a sliver of light from the gaslights above. After what seemed like an eternity, Hero returned. "If you think you are leaving me here, you are mistaken." He climbed down the ladder. When he reached the bottom, Edward pulled his match safe and struck a match. Hero put the tip of a lamplighter's wick into the flame. "I have no intention of getting lost down here in the dark, so I swiped a wick from a nearby lamplighter station."

Edward smiled in the dim light. What little he could see of the passage was clear, with a bit of water dripping and rocks jutting from the earthen walls. The walkway ended at the ladder and led in a southerly direction toward the church. *At least that is a good sign*, Edward thought.

The match burned his fingers, and he dropped it. He ran his right hand along the wall and proceeded several hundred feet, with Hero holding the lamplighter behind him. His breath sounded as if it were booming, and when he held his breath, he could hear his heart beat. The passageway became rockier and more hazardous. They carefully picked their way through another few hundred feet of excavated tunnel before the passage changed and both the walls and the floor transitioned to smooth limestone. He had not realized it before, but looking back, he could see they were descending deeper into the earth. They walked single file through the humid tunnel for several minutes. Edward could hear more water dripping nearby, but that seemed to be the only sound besides their own breathing.

They came around a bend, and Edward noticed two flickering torches in the distance. He instructed Hero to stay well behind the corner and snuff their torch. Hero did, and they carefully made their way toward the lights, feeling their way. They reached a place where there was a wide stream with a small platform dock lit with two flaming torches. They waited to see if anyone was around, but after fifteen minutes, they saw no one.

"We need to get over there," Edward said. He led Hero along the bank upstream for a few more minutes until they came to a foot-bridge across the stream. It seemed sound, so they walked across and proceeded back downstream on the other side to the dock, where the room opened considerably. They huddled in a dark section of tunnel, waiting again to see if anyone was there. They realized they were alone, despite the lit torches and it felt safe to move on.

They walked past the two large pillars carved into the rock into what appeared to be an enormous ballroom of stone. The ceiling was at least twenty feet above them, and the walls were barely visible in the dim light. There was a narrow-gauge railroad track that led away from the pillars into the darkness. Edward used a torch to relight the lamplighter, and they followed the track, which appeared to be recently used, judging by the lack of rust or dust on the rails. The wall beside them was smooth limestone with divots where blocks had been cut away. There were words written in charcoal on the walls, mostly names and dates. As they walked, Edward saw an elaborate sketch on the wall of columns and archways. He stopped to look at it and realized it was the engineer's construction drawing for the room they were in. Unfortunately it did not give details beyond the area they could already see.

They came to an intersection with another tunnel. The new tunnel was smaller and cut at a ninety-degree angle to the tunnel they were in. Edward's stomach clenched. *It would be extremely easy to get lost in here.*

He turned to Hero. "Do you have anything we could use as a marker?"

Hero bent over and picked up a small black rock. "Here. See if this will mark the wall so we know the way out."

Edward scratched it on the wall and left a clean white line, which he figured would have to do, then said, "I see a small light down this side tunnel. We should go that way." He snuffed their torch again, and they crept toward the next light.

Closer to the light, they could see there was an opening in the rock, like a small room on one side. They shuffled as quickly as possible. When they got to the opening, Edward quietly moved away from the wall and looked deeper into the room.

Inside, a man sat at a table playing solitaire. A massive wooden door was behind him. Edward drew his gun, and Hero did likewise. They approached the man.

"Stay quiet and we will not hurt you," Edward said.

The man held up his hands. Hero walked behind him and pistol-whipped his head. The man crumpled into a heap, and they carried his body back into the dark corridor.

Edward and Hero returned to the small room and removed the cards which might have alerted someone else passing by that the man was missing. Edward held his finger to his lips and pointed to the wooden door at the back of the room. Pressing his ear to the door, he heard nothing. He opened it to find a dark tunnel with a banging noise coming from some distance away.

Chapter Forty Five

E dward retrieved the torch and he and Hero continued toward the noise coming from the tunnel. Farther from the river, the ground rose sharply. They passed from the narrow tunnel to larger rooms with columns and block archways. As they moved through, Edward made scorch marks on the walls with the torch to ensure they could find their way out. There were few side passages, and all seemed dark and disused, so they continued along the rail line.

"What is the purpose of these rails?" Edward wondered.

Hero laughed. "Moving items to and from the church? The rails are shiny and area obviously still used for something."

As they continued walking, they saw a distant light down the line and snuffed their torch. They crept away from the rail line and crouched. They heard the squeal of wheels on the track getting louder.

Hero whispered to Edward, "I guess we shall see what they use on the track."

It seemed an eternity of waiting as the sound rang louder through the tunnel. When it finally neared them, they could see it was a handcar being operated by four men followed by three pallet cars stacked with closed crates.

After they passed, Edward remarked, "They must be making a shipment. We should investigate where they came from while they are gone." Hero agreed, and after the rail cars had gone out of sight, they relit their torch and moved as quickly as they could.

It was not long before they saw several carbide lights blazing in the darkness. They doused their torch again and moved in slowly. There were two men in the room, which was reasonably well lit. Edward and Hero watched as the men moved among several stacks of crates. Edward and Hero both drew their guns, and Edward said, "There may be more men nearby, so let us get these two done as quietly as we can."

Edward stole up behind the first man and knocked him out with the butt of his gun. The man grunted as he went down, but his compatriot did not seem to notice. They crept to the second man, where Hero did the honors and knocked him out quickly.

They listened for a moment to see if anyone else was around, but all remained quiet. They picked up the bodies and carried them behind a stack of crates at the back of the room, where Edward noticed another door. Above it was an inscription: *Prohibere! Hoc est imperium mortis.* Edward translated in a whisper, "Stop! This is the Empire of Death." Hero nodded, and they positioned themselves to shoot whoever might be inside—or at least threaten them into compliance. Edward knew shooting would bring everyone running, and he hoped to avoid that.

He opened the door but before he could enter, a chair flew at his head and knocked him flat onto his back.

Catherine and Evaline raced out. with Evaline brandishing a chair and Catherine brandishing a torch. Then they recognized Hero.

Catherine's eyes locked on Edward laying prone in the dust. "Edward, oh my goodness! Edward, I am so sorry! Thank God it is you!"

Edward smiled as he got to his feet. "Thank God it is you! We need to get out of here before anyone notices you are gone."

He looked into the room where Catherine had been imprisoned. Hundreds of skulls lined the walls. There were two chairs with rope discarded near each one. He gasped and put his hand to his mouth, then turned to Catherine.

"The sooner we are away from this place, the better," she said.

They walked up the passageway, Catherine tightly gripping Edward's left hand while his right held one of the carbide lights. When they came to the crossroads with the side corridor, Edward suggested they wait there for the train to pass again, since it was likely the crew was at the dock loading a boat. The others agreed, and they drew the covers on their carbide lights. As they stood in the dark waiting, Edward could feel Catherine shivering. He put his arms around her, held her tightly to him in the dark, and kissed her hair.

It was five minutes later when they heard the train wheels again. Catherine shook more violently. "It is all right. No one will hurt you. I am here," he whispered.

She buried her face in his chest, quivering as the train passed. Once it had, they pulled back the covers of the lights and raced down the corridor as fast as they could. They slowed as the path sloped down toward the stream to not lose their footing. When they reached the room with the dock, Edward noticed there were no torches. He assumed the crew had made their last run for the night. Edward could smell fresh air and cigarette smoke. He stopped for a moment.

Phillipe Vardell stepped out of a recess in the rock, pointing a gun at him. "And where do you think you're going? Put your weapons on the ground."

Edward threw his light at Phillipe, but he dodged it and shot at Edward. The bullet missed, but the sound was deafening and Catherine stood screaming with her hands over her ears. Evaline also had her hands over her ears, but she was huddled into a small ball.

Edward shook his head from the ringing in his ears as Phillipe said again, "Put down your weapons!"

Hero and Edward both put their guns down and kicked them toward Phillipe.

"I thought you were helping us. I thought you worked for Alfonse. Who the hell are you?" Edward asked.

"I am a Prussian of little consequence trying to secure the greatest discovery of modern warfare for my government." Phillipe picked up their guns.

Edward asked, "Why kidnap Catherine?"

Phillipe smiled. "That was an accident. Kidnapping the daughter of one of the world's largest shipping magnates was never part of the plan, but our operatives were unsure which woman was Evaline, so they brought them both. When we discovered who we had on our hands, we realized we had a golden opportunity."

"Excuse me? How?"

"It is such a pity that Pieter Haas escaped from prison, kidnapped the ladies, and killed you all. I am certain your respective governments will want justice for such an act. Prussia will have allies in France and England to defeat Denmark and perhaps even take more of their land."

"Why are you doing this? You have the formula from Herr Nobel. Why kidnap anyone?"

"We wanted to be sure we had all copies of Davet Molyneux's notes. Madame Molyneux likely has knowledge of this work that she still has not divulged. Miss Briggs was just an unfortunate casualty of this whole affair. Or will be."

"You killed Chloe."

Phillipe laughed. "Indeed I did. Along with Davet and your friend Henri. Poor bumbling fool; he thought he could stop us. Von Bismarck wanted everyone besides Herr Nobel who had been involved killed. That way, no one could have the formula except Prussia. Chloe was trying to sell her knowledge of the formula to Pieter Haas. I do not know how much she told him, but you releasing him has made my work much harder. I do not appreciate it."

Edward heard someone behind him, then he felt a sharp blow to the back of his head. He was out like a light.

Chapter Forty Six

When Edward awoke, his vision was fuzzy, but he saw Catherine leaning over him. She was stroking his head, which was in her lap. He could hear the echoes of her voice: "…He is waking up…" The rest was garbled, and he closed his eyes as he felt her stroking his cheek and whispering something unintelligible.

When his eyes opened again, he did not know how long it had been since the last time he had seen her. He gazed about and saw Hero and Evaline with them. He tried to sit up, but Catherine pushed him down.

"Stay put. You suffered a nasty blow. Can you hear me?"

"Yes, I can hear you and see you as well. Where are we?"

"Back in the ossuary."

Edward slowly tried to sit up, and Catherine tried to stop him. Edward protested. "No, let me get up, please. We need to find a way out of here."

Hero said "We have been working on that. I cannot find any other way out of here but that door."

Edward rubbed his head and stared at the floor for a long, silent moment. He recalled Phillipe Vardell saying he had killed Henri, and his blood boiled. He wanted revenge, and the only way to get it was to get free. Edward glanced around, but all he saw were bones, long bones: femurs, tibias, humerus bones, skulls, ulnas, and vertebrae. Edward wondered where all the foot bones were, as he did not see any. He stopped and collected his thoughts for a moment, and then it came to him.

"The sign said 'Stop. This is the Empire of Death.' Seems odd that the empire should just be in this one room. Besides, outside that door is the old mine, but we know there is a catacomb beneath the church. Help me look for another passage." He stood up, swayed, and steadied himself against a shelf of skulls.

He stepped back to the wooden door and stood just below the lantern that hung above it to survey his surroundings. The walls had a base of three levels of skulls, with femurs in a layer between them. Above the top layer of femurs were alternating layers of femurs, humerus bones, and above them, a scalloped pattern created by rib bones and pelvic bones. Edward admired the artistry to create the shapes, which extended all the way around the room without a break—nothing to show where a door or passage might be. He scoured the patterns again and again, looking for any oddities.

Then he noticed it. High on the opposite wall, a single skull set in a box made of femurs with crossed tibia bones above it. He walked across the room and began disassembling the wall. The ladies gasped as he touched the bones.

Edward said, "Hero, help me. I think I have found a way out."

Hero glanced at Catherine with a wide-eyed look that questioned Edward's sanity, but he complied and began slowly removing bones. "Will touching the bones make us sick?"

"Not finding a way out will surely make us dead. These bones are old. The likelihood of illness is very slim," Edward said as he added more and more bones to the pile.

The walls were several layers of bones deep. However, there were shelves midway up the wall and another set higher up holding the uppermost bones. He worked his way deeper into the wall beneath the shelf. At one point, the surrounding bones destabilized and fell in on him. Catherine screamed and raced toward him, but he held up his hand. "I am all right. Keep listening at the door and let me know if anyone is coming."

He worked his way through the last course of bones. Behind it was a door. Edward pressed his ear to the wood and heard nothing. The lock on the door had rusted through, probably a century ago, and he cautiously opened it.

It was dark beyond the door, and the air smelled stale. Hero stood on a chair on his tiptoes to remove the lantern from above the door. Edward carried it through the doorway, plunging the room full of bones into darkness.

Catherine started to follow him. "Edward, please—"

Edward held up his hand. "I will be right back. Just close your eyes. It will only be dark in here for a moment."

He walked down the corridor for fifty feet. He felt no movement to indicate a source of fresh air. *For all I know, this could be a dead end that kills us.* Then his mind turned. *Or it may be our only means of escape.* The corridor was lined with bones. He knew getting the women through this was going to be difficult, but it was only a matter of time before Phillipe killed them all. In fact, Edward wondered why they were not dead already. He shook his head and returned to the room.

"I believe this is our only chance at escape. Ladies, I warn you, this will be unpleasant, but it is likely our only way out. If you want to close your eyes and have Hero and me guide you, we can."

"That is unnecessary," Catherine said as she lined up behind Edward. Evaline stood behind Catherine, and Hero took up the rear.

Edward led them down the passage. The walls were so narrow that occasionally the bones would snatch at the ladies' dresses, and they would gasp in horror. Edward was thankful they did not shriek. Edward looked back and saw the abject terror in Catherine's wide eyes coupled with the steel resolve in the tight set of her jaw, and he knew she would keep her wits about her. They continued on.

In some places, the ceiling was so low Edward had to duck. They passed several alcoves on either side with the names of neighborhoods from which the bones had come carved into the rock of the ceiling. Here were the bodies from Gronau, there were bodies from Beuel-Ost. Ahead he saw Endenich.

Eventually they came to an intersection. Fear gripped Edward's mind: *We could be lost under here until we die.* Suddenly the gravity of his decision to leave their prison weighed on him. *Think, Edward, think!*

He tried to construct a mental map of where they had been. They had entered from the north, then moved south toward the church, then found the intersection with the stream that flowed east to the river, then followed the railroad tracks.

Catherine said "Edward," and he raised his hand for quiet.

After a moment he said, "We go left. That should lead us to church."

They followed him for another ten minutes. At that point, the corridor widened and the alcoves were larger. Although the passages had more bones within them, they felt less cramped. The earth beneath them began to rise, and Edward felt a small flicker of hope.

After a few more minutes, they came to a door. Edward opened it slowly and peered through the crack. It was dark on the other side, deserted, but the air smelled clean. They crossed into the next room, which had smooth walls of stone and no bones. The ceiling was higher here. Once they were all through the door, Edward looked back and saw the same warning above the threshold: Stop! This is the Empire of Death.

He smiled and hugged Catherine. "We made it."

Catherine breathed a deep sigh of relief, and they shared a brief moment of quiet celebration. Well ahead of them, farther down the passage, they saw another door. Catherine said, "Hopefully that is the church."

Hero stepped forward. "Edward, we need a plan."

Edward turned back into the closest section of the ossuary and pulled two femurs from the last section of bones. "All we have are fire and bones," he said on his return. "We should make use of them."

They moved carefully forward, Edward holding Catherine's hand and Evaline holding Hero's. When they reached the large wooden door, Edward saw it was elaborately decorated with scrollwork carvings and a cross in the center. Edward listened at the door and heard nothing. Given that it was four o'clock in the morning, that seemed reasonable.

He cracked open the door and peeked through. There was a narrow set of carpeted stairs to the left and a door straight ahead. Edward found it locked. Hero instructed everyone to stay where they were, and he silently climbed the stairs. Edward, Catherine and Evaline heard a rather loud sound.

Hero came back moments later and informed them, "I have managed the guard at the top of the steps."

They raced up the steps to the crumpled guard, who had a rifle and a sidearm. Hero took the rifle, and Edward took the sidearm. They climbed two more flights of steps and entered the church just behind the right-hand dais.

Edward whispered to Hero, "Take the women and get as far away from here as you can."

"What about you?"

"I will be along shortly."

CHAPTER FORTY SEVEN

Edward watched his three companions leave the church. Hero approached all corners with his gun pointed, ready to kill anyone who threatened them. It made Edward happy that someone so soft was taking his charge so seriously.

When they had gone, Edward went on the hunt. There was no one in the church, so he went into the courtyard in the center of the complex. Covered walkways surrounded the garden, with arches along the path overlooking the garden, and there were a few gaslights ablaze. Edward skulked around the dark corners but found no one. He entered a door into a short tower at the far end of the courtyard. There were stairs going both down and up. He surmised the stairs going up went back to the bell tower, so he followed the stairs down.

He heard steps ahead. He peered over the railing to see Phillipe Vardell on the stairs below him. Phillipe fired at him. Edward pulled back, and the bullet missed. Edward heard a door open and close.

He raced down after him and listened at the door, but heard nothing. If he opened the door, he knew he risked being shot at, but he had no choice. He crouched as low as he could, opened the door, and scuttled inside as the door closed by its own force behind him. Shots rang out, and Edward heard one whiz by his head, but he was not hit. He ducked behind a large wooden table and scurried to the right.

"I will kill you, Edward. You should make your peace with God."

Edward made no sound as he took in his surroundings. Where he crouched, there were altars, some heavy and wooden, some painted white and gold, some solid marble, with chalices lined up on several altars, their shiny brass reflecting the few gas lights in the room. Farther on, there were large, shiny brass crosses all lined up in a neat row. Edward searched them for reflections of Phillipe, but saw none. *This must be some kind of warehouse for church furnishings.*

Edward crept deeper into the room, listening for his quarry. He heard footsteps to the right and moved toward them. This area was storage for statues. Mother Mary, clad in blue robes, with her face bent toward him and her eyes full of pity, stared as he passed. He shook the frisson of fear that crept up his spine and moved toward a statue of Saint Francis surrounded by lambs on a large plinth. Edward waited behind the plinth until he saw the back of Phillipe Vardell moving between pews nearby. Edward shot, but missed. Phillipe ran off between stored pews further into the room.

"You're not a very good shot, Mister Tyrington. Too bad."

Edward heard Vardell's footsteps move away, and he followed the sound toward the center of the warehouse. Edward moved past statues of Archangel Michael with huge sweeping wings, looking as though he could pluck Edward from the room and fly him straight to the heavens. *Although that would be unlikely,* Edward thought. He searched the room for signs of movement. As he moved past a painting of God and Jesus seated in heaven, a shot flew past his left ear. He ducked and scurried toward a marble baptismal basin.

He caught sight of Phillipe and fired. Phillipe howled in pain, and Edward could hear him trying to move away, as if he was dragging himself. Edward ran toward the noise.

As he passed a statue of Jesus, he heard a shot, and pain exploded in his left arm. He saw the blood erupt from his arm as he spun around from the force of it. He spotted Phillipe, who was dragging his right leg. He raised his pistol and fired.

Phillipe fell, and Edward crossed to him. Phillipe lay dying, surrounded by a dozen life-size crucifixes, Jesus's head bent under the crown of thorns and staring down at him in forgiveness and pain.

Phillipe's mouth moved, and Edward shot him again.

"That was for Henri."

Edward inspected his own arm. Phillipe's bullet had hit his forearm, but it had not hit bone. He wrapped his arm in an altar cloth and applied a tourniquet to stanch the bleeding.

He quickly moved to the door and opened it to see three men running down the stairs from above. Ducking back into the warehouse, he hid behind an altar. The men entered, and he watched as they walked deeper into the room. Before they could see him, he crept out the door and made sure it closed silently.

He knew he was low on bullets and could only fire on those who fired at him. He raced back to the courtyard. Near the door to the church, he heard voices, and he crept back into the darkness. Four men exited the church, and one said, "It sounded like shots near the bell tower." They ran in that direction.

Edward scanned the courtyard and found an exterior door. His arm throbbed in pain as he opened and fled into the church plaza, hiding in the shadows as he went.

He did not know where Hero and the ladies had gone. They could not return to the hotel, so he tried the next place that seemed reasonable.

Eventually he found the woods where Edward and Catherine had hidden after leaving Poppelsdorf Castle. Had that only been a few hours ago? He tried to tiptoe in the woods, but the crunch of leaves beneath his feet seemed inordinately loud. He heard a twig pop nearby and spun his head around.

"We are here," he heard Hero whisper.

Catherine ran toward him. "Are you all right?"

"Shhhh. We must not be found. Yes, I am fine. We need to get out of here."

"You are bleeding." Catherine held his hand and inspected his arm.

"I am shot, but I have applied a tourniquet and should be all right until we are safe."

"I sent a message to Reed," Hero said. "I told them to meet us at the park on the river."

The four of them made their way to the park. Hero went ahead alone to the meeting place while Edward, Catherine, and Evaline stayed in a copse of trees, watching. Hero met the carriage and waved for Edward's group to join him.

Edward, Catherine and Evaline quickly came over and jumped into the large carriage pulled by two horses. Reed drove them off into the night toward Cologne to the north, with Daniella riding next to him. Davis tended to Edward's wound inside the carriage; Catherine, Evaline, and Hero averted their eyes. It was a deep graze, but thankfully the bullet had not disrupted the bone or much of the muscle. He offered Edward a sedative for the pain, but Edward refused.

It was several hours before they reached Cologne, and they slept in the carriage as best they could. They left the carriage outside of town and walked to the train station, where Catherine asked for seven train tickets to Eupen.

Evaline said, "We must return to Lunéville."

Catherine asked, "Why?"

"I left something there for you. We must retrieve it."

They found a quiet corner to wait for the train, and Edward asked, "Why Eupen? I thought we were going to France?"

Catherine whispered, "They will stop us at the border. We are a fairly recognizable group. When the officers come through the train to check passports, they will arrest us. We will have to cross the frontier into Belgium on foot and travel from there."

The trip to Eupen was short. They walked to an outdoor café to eat a breakfast of sausages. They observed their surroundings as they ate, but nothing seemed out of the ordinary. It was only ten o'clock in the morning, and Edward wondered how far news of their escape and Phillipe's death would have traveled. He knew it would be suicide to assume the police did not seek them.

After they ate, they walked west to the edge of town and entered the forest. They moved deep into the woods, away from the roads that crossed into Belgium. The trees were bare, with a leaden sky weighing down on them, threatening to rain at any moment. Edward had gotten his bearings in town, but navigating under cloud cover made his job of finding the way more difficult. It had rained here, and while that kept their footsteps quiet in the wet leaves, it also made the walking muddy and slick in some places. The seven of them walked for two and a half hours, stopping periodically to allow the ladies to rest. Hero had brought a wineskin full of water to drink. It tasted awful, with the bitter musty smell of red wine tainting the freshness of the water, but they were thankful for it. Eventually they reached farmlands and followed a road into Herve. It was a small town, but it was in Belgium and away from von Bismarck's police or influence. They found a small restaurant and inn at which to dine for lunch, after which they arranged for a carriage to take them to the closest train station. They arrived at the town of Limbourg near sunset. They arranged for a hotel and Davis, Reed, and Daniella shopped for clothes.

The next morning, Edward wired Alfonse and told him to meet them in Lunéville three days hence. Edward also wired his brother Charles.

CHAPTER FORTY EIGHT

After days of travel, the party arrived in Lunéville the evening before Alfonse and Charles were to meet them.

Joelle was waiting for them at the train station, along with Evaline's family and the chief of police. Joelle greeted Edward warmly and said, "I took the liberty of ensuring the police could protect you. We still do not know who might be lurking about."

"I appreciate that. It has been quite a journey, but no one has followed us—at least, not that we could tell."

They went to the hotel to bathe and change clothes. Edward felt lighter than he had since he heard Henri was dead. Nothing would take that pain from him, but avenging his best friend did wonders for his attitude. He had shared with Catherine, in the vaguest of terms, what happened in the church that night and that he had killed Phillipe. He gave Hero and Davis the more detailed version and hoped he would not have to share the story again.

After dark, Edward, Catherine, Hero and Evaline went to the grave of Evaline's great-grandmother. Edward did the honors and dug a small hole next to her grave. About two feet down, his shovel hit a metal box. He dug it out and opened it.

Evaline said, "Davet's notes. In their entirety."

Joelle breathed a heavy sigh of relief. "This will save our entire family from Napoleon's wrath. Thank you, Evaline."

As they left the graveyard, Catherine spoke up. "It seems to me that we still have a problem."

Joelle turned to her. "How so?"

"Only two of the major powers will have this technology. This gives them an unfair advantage. Perhaps if England also has this technology it will be used less because it gives no one the upper hand."

Edward chimed in. "And it is true that two British subjects helped recover these documents. Without our efforts I am not sure we would have recovered Evaline, or the notes."

Joelle nodded. "That seems fair. I could not have recovered the documents without your help and if the threat of mutual destruction limits the use of dynamite on the battle field, then that benefits everyone. When we return to the hotel, please make the additional copy of the notes."

In the morning Alfonse and Charles arrived. Edward and Catherine presented a copy to Charles, while Joelle and Evaline presented another copy to Joelle's father.

Edward said, "Prussia has the secret of stabilizing nitroglycerin to make dynamite. These notes are the sum total of Davet Molyneux's work on the subject. We are giving these to the French and English governments so that Prussia is not the sole possessor of this technology. We believe Denmark may also have this information."

Charles was incredulous. "You are just giving this information to any government that wants it? Edward, you are my brother. Why are you giving this to Napoleon? Are you mad?"

"Because Napoleon would kill the entire le Marchal family for losing this information to Prussia if it was not recovered. Besides, it was a French scientist who discovered it. You are lucky I am here to make sure you have a seat at the table."

Charles clutched the papers tightly as he placed them in his case.

Edward walked Charles to his carriage. When they were alone, Edward said, "The Prussians kidnapped Catherine and Evaline. They wanted to frame Denmark with the crime and give themselves more support for the war they are fomenting. I know there is little you can do about that, but Catherine is a British citizen."

"Unfortunately, without hard evidence, there is little we can prove and nothing I can do. I am sorry about that."

"Also, you should know that the Prussians will accuse me of helping a man escape jail and of killing someone."

Charles looked at Edward for a long moment. "I know times have been hard for you, but are you turning to a life of crime?"

"Of course not. I was wrongly jailed. When Hero came to rescue me, my cellmate also escaped."

Charles, being more savvy than he typically let on, asked, "Who was your cellmate?"

"Pieter Haas."

Charles, who knew exactly who Pieter Haas was, smiled like the Cheshire Cat. "Is that so? Could not have happened to a nicer person. Or at least a nicely sized thorn in a certain country's backside. I assume he escaped Prussia as well?"

"I believe so."

"Very good. Who will they say you killed?"

"Phillipe Vardell, a Prussian double agent who was using connections with the French to inform the Prussians. He is the man who murdered Davet and Henri."

"Did you kill him?"

"Not that anyone saw."

"Well, if no one saw it, they have no proof that it was you. Besides, it sounds as if the world is better off without him." Charles said.

At breakfast the next morning, Edward found Evaline and Catherine speaking to Joelle. Joelle caught him up in the conversation, telling him the documents had been delivered to Napoleon.

"So we paid the debt of your family in full?"

"Yes. Thank you. We can all travel home on the afternoon train to Paris if that agrees with you."

"Quite. The sooner the better."

After they dined Edward went to the wire office and sent Bergeron a quick note:

Your missing elephants may be in Bonn, under the Munster Church.

The wire operator read it looked at him for a long moment.

"It is an inside joke."

He left with a smile on his face. He did not know if the elephants had made it to Bonn, but there was certainly a smuggling operation under that church and a storage area large enough to house such objects. If Bergeron did not find his elephants, he would likely find something else of value, and Edward would certainly rather see Bergeron have it than the Prussians.

That afternoon on the train would seem, to all observers, to be like the first day these seven had traveled together. Hero drank his wine and expounded on several new varietals that he was going to plant and showed them the cuttings he had collected on their journey. Catherine's fingers jumped through the complex knots of tatting on her lap, and Edward read the newspaper. But Edward knew nothing was the same as when they left. Now Catherine barely spoke, and the anticipation of a mystery to be solved had changed into a time to manage painful memories.

When they arrived at the Paris train station that night, Catherine gathered her belongings and raced to the exit. Even her ladies' maid, Daniella, was surprised that Catherine had already engaged a carriage before the maid could get half the bags unloaded.

Edward went to Catherine as she sat waiting for her maid. "May I share your carriage?"

"No. There is no room for your things and mine, and besides, I am pining for my father and would like to get home as soon as possible." The carriage arrived, and Daniella began loading their bags.

Edward tipped his hat. "Of course. May I call on you tomorrow?"

"You have work to catch up on, and frankly, I need to rest. Perhaps another day." Daniella finished securing the bags to the carriage, and Catherine stepped inside.

"Please rest. This has been a trying journey." Edward said through the window. She nodded, and the driver pulled them away. Edward sighed. All he wanted to do was wrap her in his arms and hold her, but that kind of sympathy was never Catherine's cup of tea, and clearly, she would avoid any sympathy or comfort from him now. His heart ached over it.

CHAPTER FORTY NINE

H e spent the next day recruiting a crew for his excavation. Most workers were happy to come back to work once they learned he was still alive, although the more superstitious ones declined the offer. That evening, they reopened the passage he had previously inspected and began their work there.

Not long after starting, they discovered a small passage that he had overlooked before. The brickwork was different, and when they pulled some bricks out, there was a passageway beyond it. It led to four rooms of bones, two on each side of the passage, and a room of skulls at the end. Tears stung his eyes as he worked in the skull room and thought of Catherine sitting with Evaline, afraid and alone in such a room, and rage filled him again. But this time the rage crystallized his mind on a single purpose, a single task he could not fail or living would no longer serve a purpose. He informed his crew he would arrive at work in the afternoon the following day. They presumed he would want to sleep after the late-night work they were performing, but he had other plans.

The following morning he had Davis dress him in his best clothes, including his father's gold cufflinks. He arrived at Catherine's house at the beginning of the morning calling hour. She invited him in, and after a few minutes of conversation, her father left the salon so they could be alone. They sat on opposite sofas and Edward bounced his knee absentmindedly as they made small talk.

Finally Edward said, "Catherine, there is a purpose to my visit today aside from inquiring about your welfare." She stared at him expectantly, and he continued. "What I mean is...well...um...I have decided something. Something of vital importance."

"Yes, what is it?"

Edward crossed the room and sat next to her on the sofa. "There are some things that cannot be denied, and the more you try, the harder your life becomes. But this is something I have been sure about for quite a while now, and nothing else will do."

"Edward, what are you talking about?"

Edward knelt before Catherine and pulled the small box from his pocket, which he opened to reveal an ornate ring. "Catherine, would you do me the honor of accepting my proposal for marriage? I do not want to spend another minute of this life without you by my side."

Catherine stood. "How could you? You know I have no intention of marrying. You do not want me as a wife—"

"I do. I want nothing else in this world—"

"No. And if you knew the truth about me, you would deem me unsuitable." She burst into tears and ran from the room yelling, "No, I cannot. I cannot."

Edward followed her to the base of the stairs to see her run up the last few steps. His instinct was to follow, but knew he could not go into her room, where she was undoubtedly headed. He called after her, "Catherine, please. Let us discuss this."

She yelled back, "No." And he heard a door slam.

He stood at the base of the stairs for a moment and looked at the box in his hand. *Of course she would never want you, Edward, you fool.*

John Briggs came out of the dining room. "Ye gods, what is going on?" As his eyes fell on the box and the ring, he said, "Oh."

Edward pocketed the box and said, "Excuse me."

John grabbed his arm. "I had hoped she would see reason, but you know how she can be. Meet me at the Lyonnaise Bistro in an hour and a half. It is of vital importance that you be there. Promise me you will."

Edward sighed. "What is the point?"

"Promise!"

"All right, I promise I will be there."

"Good. Now let me attend to my hardheaded daughter. I will see you soon."

Edward left and wandered the streets of Paris. He scratched a note for a runner to take to the archaeological site saying that he would not be working today. He instead went to the Seine, where he walked for an hour along the river. He wept openly and did not give a damn who saw him. There would be no wife for him. How could there be? No other girl was half the woman she was. Her bravery, her cunning, her incredibly sharp mind—no one else would do. He did not relish the thought of his life without her in it.

At the appointed time, he arrived at the bistro. John arrived soon after, and they took a table in the back, away from the other diners.

John put a small briefcase on the table. "I had hoped to never look at these again, but it seems we must. But before we do, I want to say that I thought Catherine was changing her mind about you. You told me you were betrothed, but I knew you were not. Not really. But I also thought that allowing Catherine to spend time with you without the weight of an impending engagement might open her mind to the idea. When she chose Hero as her chaperone for your trip, I was sure she was in love."

"Why?"

"Let me make some guesses as to your journey with Hero, and you can tell me if I am right or not. As soon as your train arrived, he left you both to your own devices because he had made plans to see someone else."

Edward's jaw fell open. "Yes."

"After that, he was more absent than present and consistently found opportunities to be in other places, even in towns where it seemed no one knew who he was."

"Yes."

"That is how he operates. So Catherine choosing him as her chaperone meant she was very comfortable with you. That she trusted you implicitly."

"Then why refuse my proposal?"

He opened the case, pulled out several newspapers, and put them on his lap. "Before I show you these, I must explain what happened, because the newspapers did not get the details right. Did you ever wonder why Catherine and I live in Paris?"

"Not really. Usually a reversal of fortune causes an Englishman to move to France. But clearly that is not the case for you."

"In my case, it was the murder of my wife."

Edward tilted his head. "I thought you said she died of an illness."

"I lied. It was a rather famous case; you will probably remember it, although you were rather young at the time. It was ten years ago in March. A man broke into our house and murdered my wife—or at least that is the official story. Now. But initially, because I was not home, they accused Catherine of the murder. Catherine is her middle name. Her given name is Annie. Do you recall anything about Annie Briggs being accused of murder?"

"I confess I do not. As a teenage boy, I did not read newspapers as I do now."

"Annie was accused because one of her friends had hidden a penny dreadful storybook about a wicked daughter who killed her strict mother in Annie's room so that her own mother would not find it. When the murder was discovered by one of our staff, Annie was there, standing over Florence's body, her hands covered in blood. During the search, they found the book and assumed the book had given her the idea to kill her mother. Nothing could have been further from the truth, but we lived through months of hell grieving her mother and clearing Annie's name."

"Poor, dear girl."

"Please save your pity. This is hard enough to convey."

"Please continue."

"As I said, she believes these events make her unmarriageable. Hence her answer today. I know she loves you, Edward. I know it as I know my name, but she will not let this go."

"Then I will tell her I know and that I do not care, because I do not. I mean, I care that she has suffered so, but it does not matter to me in terms of whether I still want to marry her. Of course I do!"

"I understand that, and you understand that, but she feels there is a cloud over her name as an accused murderess. She refuses to relent. However, I think if you found the killer, and her name was truly cleared, that might go toward softening her stance."

"You expect me to solve a ten-year-old murder? I am sorry if this sounds indelicate, but are you mad?"

"Without a doubt. But I feel the only way she will put that chapter behind her is for her name to be cleared. Then perhaps she will listen to reason."

Edward reached for the sheaf of newspapers. "If this is what it will take to marry Catherine, then I will try. God help me, I will try."

THE END

I sincerely hope you enjoyed The Skulls of Malgrange! Please consider leaving a review for this book. You can order Book 3 of the Edward Tyrington Mysteries – The Skeletons of Harrow to find out what happens next! Finally, you can join my newsletter at www.joniswift.com where you will get the FREE prequel story – Trouble in Cadiz, info on new releases, stories and an occasional cool link.

Acknowledgements

I'd like to send a huge THANK YOU to Naomi and Kimberley who are the best proofreaders a writer could want, as well as amazing friends. I'd also like to thank my wonderful editor Kristin. None of these stories would have seen the light of day without them.

Printed in Great Britain
by Amazon